13 DROPS OF BLOOD

Compiled & Edited by
Ben Thomas & D Kershaw

by

Jodi Jensen

Beth W. Patterson
Chris Bannor
Crystal L. Kirkham
D.J. Elton
J.W. Garrett
Jasmine Jarvis
K.T. Tate
Kimberly Rei
M. Sydnor Jr.
Maxine Churchman
Nicole Little
S.N. Graves

Also available and coming soon from BLACK HARE PRESS

THIRTEEN SERIES
PANDEMIC
PASSENGER 13
QUIETUS 13
ZERO HOUR 2113
13 DROPS OF BLOOD

Twitter: @BlackHarePress
Facebook: BlackHarePress
Website: www.BlackHarePress.com

Isobel, Isobel

Course through time

I require your assistance

Isobel, Isobel

I beckon you

Bring my love to me

Jodi Jensen, 2021

TABLE OF CONTENTS

IZZY

THE LOVE SPELL

by Jodi Jensen

Izzy chose her candle with the utmost care: red, made of beeswax, and never burned. Next came the anointing with virgin olive oil. Using her fingers, she pulled the oil from the top to the middle, then from the bottom to the middle until the whole thing was anointed.

She picked up her athame. After consulting the grimoire of her seventeenth century Scottish ancestor, Isobel, she started on the carvings. His name at the top, each line drawing down and stopping at the centre. *Enzo*—she smiled at the mere sight of her beloved's name. Now, hers at the bottom, every line drawing up and stopping in the middle. Between their names, she carved Celtic love knots.

When she finished, she placed the candle on the palm of her right hand, stretched her left hand out, palm up, and closed her eyes. She visualised Enzo, walking towards her, his body strong and lithe rather than broken and bloody as she'd last seen him. She'd already asked forgiveness for what she'd done, so now, the imagined look on his face was one of love and acceptance. Harnessing that love, she wrapped both hands around the candle and let the energy pour into the warm, slick wax, then placed the candle into a lovely wrought iron pentagram holder.

With her candle fully charged and ready, it was time to evoke the necessary protection for her spell. She glanced at the grimoire again, hoping her Gaelic was up to the task, hoping *she* was up to the task.

Thirteen candles.

Izzy retrieved the long tapers and lit them around the room, then went and got her round mirror. Setting the mirror in the centre of the floor, she placed her love candle and holder in the middle. Next was the salt. She spread a circle of salt around the mirror, leaving plenty of room for herself to sit inside. Once she'd opened the circle of salt, she brought the tapers, one by one, and splashed melted wax on the mirror, then lined the candles around the outside of the circle.

Sitting cross-legged in front of the mirror, she waited quietly until the melted wax dried, then picked up her athame once again. This time she carved the name

Isobel Gowdie—the Scottish witch. She held the blade in one hand and lit the love candle, focusing all of her energy on the flame. In her mind's eye, Enzo came towards her, a smile on his face and love shining in his eyes.

She sat, unmoving, until the love candle self-extinguished, then slid the blade of her athame across the palm of her hand. As blood welled, she squeezed her hand in a fist, held it over the mirror, and recited the chant.

Isobel, Isobel
Course through time
I require your assistance
Isobel, Isobel
I beckon you
Bring my love to me

A dark orb rose from the mirror...then another...and another...

Izzy watched as orb after orb left through the opening in her salt circle. Her heart leapt into her throat as the orbs kept coming. Her gaze flew to the grimoire, landing on a single phrase. *A drop of blood*—she glanced at the mirror, counted the drops...eleven...twelve...

She jerked her hand away as the last drop plopped on the surface…thirteen…

Bloody fucking hell…

She leapt to her feet and spun around to find Enzo, and twelve other figures, there, but not there. Transparent. Feet not quite touching the floor. And looking pissed as hell.

ISSA

THE ROCKED CRADLE

by S.N. Graves

After the fall...

The last notes of *Happy Birthday* petered out as Tobin's wailing once again ruined everything. As if Siobhan hadn't enough reasons to drink today, Joe's little crotch maggot of doom was, as always, inconsolable.

"My goodness." Joe scooped the birthday boy up from his highchair, bringing the child into the cradle of his arms for a soothing bounce. "It's just singing, buddy."

She washed down her husband's giddy pacification of the infant with a near-choking gulp of wine. How Joe could be so endlessly cheerful, so full of adoration for a creature that only took and screamed and *needed* 24/7, she'd never know. No getting it twisted—she loved their son. Just not so much *today.*

Today, painful memories and his shrill keening

urged her to grind his chubby little face down into the cake until his earsplitting wails turned to drowning gurgles, and those gurgles to blessed silence. But thank God for the wine, she didn't. Cheap, tepid wine that she refilled her glass with for the umpteenth time. "You shouldn't coddle him."

"Nonsense. It's his birthday." He continued to bounce the boy and rock him, Joe's family flocking around to make token efforts to cheer the child with silly faces and coos. "Besides, coddling is what babies are for."

"And *that's* why he's such a brat." Siobhan set her glass on the cluttered dining table and blew out the candle. Then took up the butcher knife to cut the cake. A cake shovel would have worked better, made it easier to flop the sugary lumps onto paper plates without making a crumbly, globby mess, but Joe didn't believe in the sanctity of kitchen tools. The proper serving knife was likely in the garage somewhere, used as a cement trowel, or duct-taped into some piece of machinery to serve as a jerry-rigged replacement part. Gone forever to Joe's whimsy.

"I think your woman needs a nap," Jeff, a brother-in-law, said, voice pitched high with birthday balloon helium. Then through an Elmo over Joe's shoulder,

"Bitch is cranky."

"Don't need a nap. Needs a dick," another brother interjected from across the room. "I know she cut you off, man, but do it for the kid. Take one for the team."

Joe chuckled nervously, nuzzling Tobin's hair and using the infant as a shield. "Guys, c'mon. You trying to get me killed?"

"I'd never kill you, Joe." Cake sliced up as neatly as it was going to get with a butcher knife, she met her husband's gaze and dragged the blade across her deft tongue in two quick swipes, stripping it of icing. "Not with witnesses."

"Just make him disappear, right, Shiv?" Jeff had abandoned the Elmo and playful tone, his gaze full of open accusation. "Like Issa, right?"

Silence consumed the room, sucked out all the air until Siobhan thought she might choke. Then someone hissed with the sting of the comment, and another dared a muttered "ouch." Siobhan couldn't find her tongue, not before Joe handed Jeff a slice of cake with a limply admonishing, "That's not funny."

Siobhan begged off the rest of the gathering in favour of crawling into bed with her phone. Wine migraine, she'd said. The party carried on without her—

loud, obnoxious, occasionally destructive—the brothers practically bounced off the hallway walls in their roughhousing. The house trembled with it, sending knickknacks toppling and family photographs along the interior wall askew.

The big portrait in the centre had now gone cockeyed.

It was the three of them—Joe and Shiv, shoulder to shoulder, Issa leaning back in Shiv's arms. Issa was only four months pregnant in that one, hardly showing at all. She'd been such a slight thing, though when the pregnancy overtook her, she'd been more like a turtle stuck on its back most of the time. By month seven, that tiny bit of pudge Siobhan clasped her hands over in the photograph had become a monstrous swell of taut, pulsating flesh.

Sometimes a tiny foot would press against Issa's stomach, leaving an imprint of the kicking beasty inside her. Sometimes it was a hand, as if Tobin was trying to claw his way out of her. Joe found this delightful, and Issa had always caressed the throbbing prints, teasing the baby's foot or aligning her palm to his.

"Look, Shiv," Issa would say. "He's waving at you. Saying 'Hi, mommy!'" She'd bring her hand to her belly to wave along with the trapped babe, her smile ridiculous and beautiful and everything Shiv loved about her. "Don't you wanna touch it, Shiv? Wanna say hi?"

"No," Shiv had said more than once. "No, I fucking do not."

Issa would pout, and that would always make Shiv's chest clench, but *she'd* never asked for this. She wasn't maternal. In fact, babies tended to give her the creeps. Her only solace was knowing it wouldn't be a little wriggly maggot forever—a few years at most, right? And more importantly, back then, it eventually had to get out of Issa's body and give Shiv her girlfriend back.

Tossing her phone to the mattress, she pushed up from the bed and crossed the floor to set the photo straight. She ran her hand along several others as well, levelling them out until she was satisfied, only to have someone crash into the hallway again.

Issa, nuzzling a set of kittens they'd fostered last summer, popped off the wall, hit the corner of the dresser, and shattered all over the floor.

Shiv flung the door open and stepped into the hall, now in complete disarray. When she roared, "That's *enough!*", Joe and his brother were wrestling so close that her voice alone was sufficient to send them both ducking for cover. "Party's over. Home *now*. All of you."

"But Shiv…" Joe shrugged off the bulk of his brother, looking to her like some chastised five-year-old sent to his room without dinner. "I *live* here?"

"You want to keep doing so? Clean up the damn mess and shut this shit down."

"Yes, sir." Joe stood straight, sighing as if he'd some right to the exasperation he exuded, and pushed his fingers through his hair to set the dishevelled mess somewhat right.

An uneven chorus of mocking "yes sirs" made its way through the house, though Shiv was positive it wasn't Joe they were mocking. She returned to bed, resisting the urge to slam the door behind her.

"I don't know why you've got to be so mean." Joe leaned against the door frame, hands in the pockets of his cosy cotton house pants, all his overexuberance drained away along with the guests in their home. Given the hour he was waking her, Shiv was fairly certain he'd finally cleared out all the family and "friends."

"You know what's mean?" she rumbled into her pillow, catching a deep stretch before squinting up at him and the glare backlighting him from the hall. "Filling the house with your people, people who fucking hate me, then expecting me to play happy host."

"You could at least *try* to be civil. They don't hate you, Shiv. They all just know how little you like them."

Her lips vibrated with the huff of unamused air she released as she pushed up from the bed and slung the blankets off. "You give them way too much credit."

"Hell, half the time I question if you like *me*."

"Just half?"

"Look, I know you miss her. *I* miss her too. You can't keep being like this, though. It's not fair to the baby, and…it's not fair to me." He shoved off the door, crossing the floor to flop on the bed so hard it nearly launched Shiv off—would have, had she not grabbed his thigh and gripped tightly. Before she could get an inch of distance, his arms were around her, pulling her close and nuzzling kisses to her neck. "Not fair to you either. Things changed. Things changed bad. Doesn't mean we don't deserve to be happy, eventually."

"I'm not mourning, Joseph." She pressed a hand to his face and pushed until he let up, until his lips couldn't reach her and his arms strained around her and gradually dropped away. "I'm not sad. I'm angry. I'm tired. And I'm not cut out for this mother shit."

He looked positively sullen, sitting there with his hands now folded in his lap, staring off into the room's shadows. "I leave for Tampa in about an hour. Jeff is taking me to the airport. Do I need to call someone to watch the baby, or can—"

"I can watch our kid."

"You don't seem to be in the best place for it right now. I can call—"

"What, Joe? You afraid I'll bash his little brains in? Hmm? Drown him when he gets on one of his wailing jags? Maybe toss him in the soundproof freezer and forget about him?"

He looked at her again, eyes wide. "Well...I *wasn't* worried."

"Kid'll be fine, man. Go to your office. Do what you do. We're all good here."

"I'm concerned for *you*. You're not yourself, Shiv."

Joe was so clueless. She had nothing more to say, and the withering look she fixed on him seemed adequate enough when he threw up his hands and left the bed.

"All right. I'm out. I'll be back in a week. Please call me if you need me. I'll come back, cut it short. Okay?"

He stood there, and it took a moment for Shiv to realise he would continue to do so until she gave him something. With a roll of her eyes and dismissive wave, she mumbled, "Yeah. Sure. Go on."

And then she was alone.

Tobin was crying. Screaming until it seemed his lungs would rupture. Shiv pulled a pillow over her head and tried to wait it out. Joe couldn't have been gone more than an hour.

"Shut up, you little mutant." She groaned into her pillow, fully prepared to will herself deaf and catatonic.

Something cold nudged beneath her toes, writhing, and she flung the covers off and threw herself from the bed so quickly she nearly landed face-first on the carpet. She jammed her fingers between the toes of her left foot, feeling for the bug, tick, spider…a roach? Nothing. Maybe she'd been half-asleep and dreaming still. She turned up the light at the bedside table and ran her hand over the sheets. There was nothing there.

Until there was…

A tiny white blob wriggled where her feet had been. She'd almost missed it, but now that she noticed it, she couldn't take her eyes off it as it flipped and flopped and inched around the clean sheets.

A maggot.

How the hell had a *maggot* got into bed with her? She let out a disgusted yell and shivered like a sopping dog trying to violently eject the wet from its fur. She searched the bed after that, but only found the one; one was enough to have her stripping the sheets and climbing into the shower.

Still Tobin screamed.

"I'm coming, you little menace!" But not until she was washed. Not until the phantom tickles of non-existent bugs creeping over her skin had been thoroughly washed away. With the shower on, she could no longer hear the child's wailing fit. She closed her eyes and submerged herself under the fall of water, letting the heat prickle her face and saturate her hair. It was the most relaxed she'd felt all day—Joe out of the house, the brat effectively silenced. She could almost drift to sleep right where she stood. Instead, she washed her hair and scrubbed her face, then opened her mouth to let the hot water flush over her teeth and tongue.

Something thick and slimy slid down her throat, squishy but firm enough to offer resistance against her swallow, like a bloated raisin.

Her gag reflex brutally kicked back at what might have been a chunky piece of animal fat. She could feel it lodged halfway down her oesophagus and bent double, hacking and tearing up, nearly vomiting in an effort to expel whatever had shot down into her. Her mind instantly went to the worst possible places for what it could be in there, and as it twisted and wriggled the possibilities darkened. Had she washed a spider into her mouth? Swallowed a greenfly?

Deep down, she already knew.

With a choking sob, the clump flew out and smacked the shower wall, sticking there a moment before slowly tumbling down the wet wall like a sticky, drunken slug.

Another maggot, this one more than a centimetre long, fat and white and stinking of death. She tore the vinyl curtain down getting free of the shower. Her whole body shook as she tied on a towel and fled the bathroom.

Tobin's yowl was nerve shattering, piercing in his pitch and terror. A disgusting flash of imagery—a dirty, painful thought of the baby in his crib, surrounded and being picked to pieces by a horde of insects—stuttered her steps to her bedroom, and she course-corrected to the nursery. The light was already on—left so by Joe, no doubt—and the child was standing in his crib, gripping the rail with one hand and reaching out to her with the other.

His cries had taken form, a rapid and panicked litany of "Mum, mmmum, mum."

"I'm here. Right here." As she reached for him,

something cold and oozing squished beneath her foot, and her next step sent her sliding. The earth yanked beneath her, room spun. She slipped in the squish and fell. The corner of the dresser seemed to launch right into her face, and her head bounced off it before the whole of her crashed into the nursery floor.

"Mum, mmmum, mum."

"Mom's here…" But she was currently flat on her ass, bleeding all over his teddy bear-skin rug. She didn't move for several moments once she landed, taking inventory of herself. Her towel was gone, unwrapped from her body and trapped beneath her. Wet warmth poured down her face from the split in her scalp. With a groan, she lifted her hand to the wound, the world spinning around her. Little bits of sticky rice fell from her fingers and trickled down her face. A piece stuck to her lip, then wriggled its way inside her mouth and along the track of her gums.

Not rice. More maggots. The squish. Everything was a blur now, but the floor crawled with milky-pale life. They made little ticking sounds as they squiggled over each other, driven to a feeding frenzy over the smell of her blood they swam in.

"Mum, mmmum, mum. Mumma!"

He wasn't reaching for her. He hadn't even noticed

her fall. No, he was reaching beyond her, and her gaze sluggishly shifted until Issa's face blocked out everything else, pressed so close to her own, near nose to nose. The creamy pallor of her eyes burning right through Shiv—more maggots danced there, sliding in and out of her nostrils, pushing up the lids of her eyes to crawl through the white pus jello filling the socket.

"Issa?"

The corner of a black lip drew up over a dirt-and-larvae-encrusted smile. "Shivvy."

꩜

Before...

"I don't know how to do this. Don't even know how to begin." Issa hugged her massive belly, every step an almost-painful-to-watch waddle as the woman paced back and forth in the nursery.

"Do what?" Shiv sat in the old-timey rocking chair Joe and Issa insisted they would need when the baby arrived. It was all wood and uncomfortable as hell, but there was nowhere else to sit in the unfinished room, so she'd plopped down there when Issa's new meltdown kicked off. She rubbed her brow in controlled frustration and sighed. "The baby? It's begun already. It's done, sweetheart. You've done it now."

"No, not Tobin. Us. I don't know how to fix *us*." Issa

stopped her pacing and threw up her hands. "I thought we'd always be a happy family. I didn't expect perfect, Shiv, but I thought we could at least be honest with each other."

"What are you talking about? Who hasn't been honest?"

"Don't. I know, okay?" The sunflower-gold baby doll dress she wore had a single pocket. Since Issa had decided to boycott pants in the last month, that pocket was stuffed to bulging with everything she might need at any given moment—candy, lip balm, the phone she pulled forth now, sending spent caramel wrappers fluttering to the floor. She paid them no mind, brushing her fingertip against her phone screen until she found what she was looking for and held it out for Siobhan to see.

She had pictures of Shiv with Owen. Specifically, a picture of them having lunch across town, leaned into each other at a table outdoors, lips pressed together in a shameful kiss. Shiv watched the picture change to another shot, and another still. There was no playing that off as anything over than what it was.

"This is going to break Joe's heart."

"Were you following me? You've been on bed rest. You aren't even supposed to be driving, but you're out *stalking* me?"

Issa shook her head and sniffled, pulling the phone back to re-examine the images herself. "Jeff was out that way. Came upon you by accident. He sent me the pictures."

"Fucking Jeff."

"He could have sent them to Joe, but he didn't. He wanted to give us a chance to deal with it. Give you a chance to come clean."

"This is some bullshit. *So what*, I had lunch. So fucking what, I kissed a guy. It was nothing. I was bored and lonely and—"

"I saw the texts on your laptop. This was not the first time you met him. And it went well beyond a kiss." Issa pushed the phone back into her bottomless pocket. "He's not even the *only* guy, Shiv."

No, Owen hadn't been the only guy. He'd been the only one she'd seen more than once. He'd been what she needed, a palliative balm to the restless ache that had consumed her of late. No, she didn't love him, but she liked him okay, and he saw her, really saw her—something Joe and Issa had been unable or unwilling to do for a long time.

At least since Tobin.

"Say something, Shiv?"

"So, you tell Joe. Right?" Shiv shrugged and shook her

head hard. "Tell him, I pack my shit, and then he's all yours. You get everything you want. The whole happy-family package, minus the cheating whore of a wife. That about sum it up?"

"No. No, no, no." For a woman so uncoordinated with her new bulk, Issa moved quickly, coming to kneel before Shiv in the rocking chair. Her eyes glossy with tears, her fingers shaking as she took Shiv's face in her hands. "The whole *happy-family package,* that doesn't exist without you. You get that?" Then she leaned in, pressing her lips to Siobhan's in a soft, lingering kiss.

Shiv indulged it—how could she not? The sweetness of the woman's lips had a way of undoing Shiv down to her very fabric. And how long had it been since she'd been able to taste her, more than casual pecks in passing in the hall? She slipped her fingers into Issa's honey-brown hair and locked her in that kiss, stealing sips of her even after Issa's sniffles forced her to pull back.

"I love you. Joe loves you." Issa spoke softly but with absolute certainty, her brow pressing to Shiv's as she slipped an arm about Shiv's shoulders and more completely melted against her. "This is something we can work through. We can do it together."

Shiv deflated, resigned, but continued to nip at Issa's lips, nuzzling along her jaw as she breathed in the sugary scent of marshmallow and lily of the valley on her skin. "Joe's never gonna go for that."

"Yes, he *will*. Unless he's willing to live without all of us, he'll forgive you."

"You mean that, don't you?" Shiv withdrew, just enough to search the other woman's gaze, to read the love and sincerity in her eyes. "You'd really…take my side over his?"

"It's not about sides. It's about choosing the family. As long as we're all together, there's nothing we can't move past, can't forgive."

Shiv brushed Issa's hair back from her tear-streaked face, collecting some of the salty moisture on the pad of her thumb for Issa to see. "You sure about that?"

"Yeah, smartass." Issa's laugh was rough with tears, but her smile was as bright and reassuring as she settled against her heels and wiped her face of tears. "I am."

But Issa was wrong.

All her accounts were tied to Joe's. All her investments were in Joe's business. All her friends were Joe's, her family was Joe's. She'd given up one hundred percent of herself to be part of this world with him and Issa, and a few moments of weakness, a few personal indulgences, were going to cost her the whole world.

Joe would be home tomorrow. Issa would tell him

everything tomorrow. Her marriage would be over…tomorrow.

She'd just wanted to feel wanted again, wanted to matter again, even if for a little while. "I can't talk you out of telling him, can I?"

"It's the right thing to do. You know that. We'll wait until he gets home this weekend. We'll tell him together."

Issa didn't know Joe the way Shiv did. It was one thing to agree to an additional lover in the group, but it was quite another to step out entirely. Joe wouldn't forgive that. Not easily. "I can't. He's going to *hate* me."

"He might…for a little bit, but I'm going to be right there with you. I know why you did it. With this pregnancy and him gone all the time, I know you feel abandoned. I know what it's like to be alone and…not sure if you matter. I hate that you did it, but…I understand why. I'll be better, Shiv. I've been lost in my own head, and I'll work on that. I won't leave you feeling all alone again. And we'll talk to Joe about these stupid trips to Tampa. Once every six months is fine, it's what we signed on for, but he's gone more often than not lately, and that is unacceptable."

Siobhan's smile was suddenly irrepressible; it made her jaws ache. She ran her hand through Issa's hair again, stroking her like some well-loved pet for several heartbeats before she slid from the rocking chair, settling against Issa to straddle her thighs.

"Wait, what are we doing?" Issa's laugh was unsure as Shiv began pushing her back, as she took hold of one foot and then the other to stretch them out behind her so she could trap Issa beneath her without putting undue strain on her enormous belly.

Issa went along easily, collapsing against the white teddy bear rug that separated them from the hardwood. "I'm as big as a moose! I'll never get up from this floor."

Shiv was undeterred. She kissed Issa's neck, pushed her shirt aside to nip and lave at her shoulder, her collarbone. Issa seemed perfectly content, chuckling softly, all loving smiles as she melted there under the onslaught of Shiv's affection. Her fingers combed through Shiv's feathery bob cut, massaging her nape as Shiv carried those reverent kisses down the length of Issa's body.

"You're going to have to drag me to bed by a fat, swollen ankle," Issa said.

"I'll help you get up." Shiv nipped at that big belly, lifting her gaze to find Issa's as the corner of her mouth tugged up in a smirk. "When I'm done."

"Ha! You have a bulldozer? Hiding a forklift somewhere I'm not privy to?"

Shiv sighed, pausing her affections to lean on an

elbow and fix the woman with a disapproving stare.

"Don't look at me like that. *You* did this." Issa poked a fingertip to Shiv's forehead accusingly. "This is me now. I'm a floor mat. An enormous, round, pregnant, floor ma—"

Siobhan dipped her head with snakelike speed between Issa's thighs, teeth rasping against Issa's baby-blue cotton panties. Shiv's playful growl was drowned out by the volume of Issa's bubbling laughter, laughter that turned into a heady moan when Shiv's thumb hooked in the hem of Issa's underwear, tugging it aside to allow her to drag the tip of her tongue up the length of her slit.

Issa's shudder was echoed in Shiv's own, and she practically purred against the woman's nuzzled sex as Issa's fingers tightened in her hair.

"Shiv…" Issa's voice was breathy. "This is the baby's room."

Shiv lifted her head, nipped at Issa's wrist, and once more met her gaze. "Not for another two weeks."

Shiv basked in the afterglow. She wasn't sure where all their clothes had landed, cradling Issa against her as she listened to the woman's breathing. These days, Issa was too uncomfortable in her own skin to tolerate much holding, touching, intimate contact at all.

It had been forever since last they'd just been able to enjoy the shared nearness. She wanted nothing more than to savour it while it lasted, fearful of breathing too hard or making an off sound that could send the woman running.

And yet...

"This is the most unromantic rug ever." Shiv lay stretched over the plushie bear, flicking a blunt nail at one of its fuzzy round ears. The thing stared at them with its bulbous, plastic eyes all googly and felty pink tongue lolled to the side of its mouth like Muppet roadkill.

"It's the baby's rug." Issa snuggled in closer, chilly fingers entwined at her chest, trapped between them. "Not supposed to be romantic. Just cute."

Cute it was not. Comically grotesque, maybe.

"I mean seriously—whose idea was it to skin the school mascot and turn him into nursery furnishing?"

"Joe found it."

"He go trophy hunting in the Hundred Acre Wood, or what? Thing could be Pooh's mentally challenged brother." Shiv grabbed it by the lopsided head and made it look directly at Issa—or as much so as its catawampus gaze could manage—and gave it her best Winnie impersonation. "Oh bother, Issa. But your honey pot is delicious!"

Issa tipped her head back with a bark of laughter, and Shiv seized on the moment to nuzzle the cold, plastic bear nose to the woman's throat.

"This isn't right, Issa." The woman squirmed and tried to respond with anything but giggles and snorts, but Shiv was unrelenting in her attack, voice gone full Muppet as she assaulted her lover with furry affection. "I'm going to frighten your children, Issa. It's like Buffalo Bill had a Care Bear fetish in here."

"Take it up with Joe!"

"Joe's a ho!"

"Stop! That's enough." Issa shifted, lumbering to sit, and then wrenched on her pullover dress without bothering to make sure it was right-side out. "Bathroom. Now. Help me up."

Shiv didn't help. She tried to reel the woman back in but was only given a quick peck on the lips, before Issa got her feet shakily beneath her. It was too soon. Whining, Shiv caught her ankle, and when Issa paused her steps and peered back at her—that grin so broad and bright it thoroughly wrecked Shiv—she brought her roadkill bear buddy back in to plead her case. "Don't leave. I can't *bear* it."

"You're an idiot. Turn me loose."

"Issa, no! Where you taking that hot snatch?"

"I have to pee. Shush!" She jerked her ankle free, shaking Shiv off. "I'll be right back."

"Oh yeah, hose it down. Only *you* can prevent bush fires, Issa."

Issa pulled her dress down into place, but with her panties tossed somewhere into the shadows of the room, her backside was still on display as she speed-waddled off.

Shiv sighed and watched her go, and the bear got his head tilted in her hands in a show of consideration. "Nice ass, goldilocks."

And Issa fell.

It was a delayed reaction, but Shiv called out and reached for her. Issa's temple had already cracked the corner of the dresser, and she spilled to the floor, a limp, shattered thing.

"Oh, shit. Oh…no." Shiv was on her in an instant, patting her face, checking her pulse, saying and then outright screaming her name. She shook her by the shoulders. She gathered up her own silk lounging shirt from the floor and pressed it to the gushing wound in Issa's head to stem the blood.

"Issa? Look at me. *Please.*"

No response.

When she groped around the woman's neck, pressing and waiting, realigning and pressing again, she felt nothing. No pulse. No breath movement. "Fuuuck, Issa. C'mon!"

Shiv fell back on her rump, bloody hands clutching her face as she stared at her lover's corpse in shock. Just like that, she was gone. Shiv'd said she would help the woman up. Why hadn't she helped her? One more little mistake and now Shiv truly was alone.

All was silence and stillness. Shiv prayed for that to change, prayed to see Issa's chest rise with breath, to hear a moan, a wheeze, any sign of life at all, but it didn't come. Not from Issa. But within her, something stirred. A little foot, and then a little hand pressed against that distended belly for escape, a parasite trying to flee a cooling corpse. Issa was dead, and Tobin was going to suffocate within her.

She was on her feet in an instant, skidding from the room and down the hall to crash into the kitchen. She flung open the utensil drawer and tossed everything in search of a sharp knife. Butter knives and spoons and a damn cake trowel they had absolutely no use for ended up on the floor. Why the hell did Joe have to make everything disappear? Every damn month they were buying new knives and spatulas because somehow, some way, the right tool for every home project in Joeland was the dinnerware they'd received on their wedding day!

She pulled the whole drawer free of its metal tracks, spilling its contents all over the floor. Maybe she could scoop the kid out with a melon baller? Before checking the garage for a box cutter, she pushed her hand through the dirty dishwater in the sink and groaned with relief as her hand drew up a butcher knife. It wasn't the best tool for the job, but it would do, and she scrambled back to the nursery and collapsed in front of the pulsating mound of belly.

She couldn't acknowledge that round form was attached to Issa. If she allowed her gaze to travel up to that pale and bloody face, she'd never be able to make the first cut, and that first cut was already almost impossible. The blade flexed as she pressed the tip into the flesh above Issa's bikini line. It wasn't like in the movies. It wasn't as easy as carving up a turkey, although that was exactly the image Shiv tried to keep in her mind as she wrestled the end of the knife under the first layer of skin, then twisted and ground and forced the knife deeper until finally blood flowed and the flesh tore under the pressure.

Tore, not cut. Sharp though the blade was, she was

practically sawing the woman open from hip to hip. The skin was thick, the muscle thicker still, and the more the blood gushed, the more difficult it was to leverage the tool. Dropping the knife, she slipped her hands inside the gaping hole, and like tearing open a particularly stubborn bag of chips, she pried the skin flap back. She had to hum to drown out the sound of moist ripping fabric, gagging at the wet squelches that followed.

The hole wasn't large enough, although she could feel movement under the slippery heat against her fingertips. There was no way she could cut the baby out without risking cutting it, so she began pulling. It was impossible to tell what was what, so she just grabbed and tugged until flesh and viscera gave way. She tore at everything that yielded in that abdominal cavity, surrounding herself with never-ending reams of slithery tubing that made it seem as if Issa had come unspooled. More than once she had to grab the knife again, gouging and ripping at that opening to get it wide enough, but finally she clawed a lumpy balloon filled with fluid and a thrashing infant through that still-too-small hole. It plopped onto the hardwood, and Shiv cut away the meaty casing wrapping the child and gave the gory bundle a few good thumps with the heel of her hand until it screamed.

And just kept screaming.

Shiv wrapped the thrashing infant in the bloody remains of her shirt and set him on the bear rug, where he flopped and writhed like an aimless maggot. Then she backed away, folded in on herself, on her knees, her fists pressed so tightly to her eyes it made them ache. For a moment she thought she might pass out.

With a single word from Issa, her body jolted alert.

"Shiv?" Issa was breathing and talking, and…breathing. Alive. Her too-pale body trembled so violently she seemed near seizures. She looked lost and terrified lying there flayed open. "Oh god, it hurts. What happened? I need…I need…Call 911."

The screaming infant was forgotten, and Shiv crawled back to Issa's side, taking her head in her hands and preventing the woman from looking down along her body to see where all that pain was coming from.

Issa swatted limply at her and tried to pull free, but Shiv held her face in a vice, her brow pressed to the woman's own. "Shhh, it's okay. Everything's going to be okay." Her tone strove for reassurance, but there was panic in her voice she could not suppress, an agony that might have rivalled Issa's disembowelment.

"Shiv, help. Help!" Her teeth chattered loudly, eyes

unfocused, desperate. "Please help?"

"You're fine. Everything is fine." With a tentative kiss to the woman's bluish lips, Shiv retracted enough to meet those terrified eyes with as much comfort as she could muster. "The baby's here and…he's fine."

"Our baby? Where?" Issa's body convulsed, arcing up from the floor as a red froth poured from the corner of her mouth. Even as her feet kicked at the hardwood, mindlessly thrashing, and her teeth clacked together so hard Shiv worried they may shatter, Issa craned her neck to seek out that wailing child. Shiv was in the way, and Issa hadn't the strength to persist. It seemed to really hit her then. Shiv could see the understanding in her eyes, could see the realisation that the chill running through her was her final moment in this world. "Did you…*kill* me? Why?"

"Shh, just shhhh, close your eyes." Shiv closed her own, biting the inside of her cheek until blood flooded her tongue and threatened to make her vomit. She could call 911. She could get help. Maybe Issa would live. Maybe she would make it to the hospital in time.

Even still, there was no coming back from what had been done here. You don't get to disembowel a woman and just go on living your life, no matter your intentions.

"Please, Shiv." Issa's convulsions abated, and Shiv held her through them, shaking her head and denying the pitiful pleas and cries of anguish. "I hurt. I'm scared. Shivvy?"

She wasn't sure when her hand had sought out the knife, but she brought it between them. With soft susurrations of love and promises that everything would be okay drowning out Issa's incoherent murmurs, Shiv fastened a hand over the woman's mouth. Those pleas, the begging and sobbing, went shrill as Shiv brought the knife down in the first stroke. She hadn't opened her eyes, so her aim was terrible, just nicking the side of Issa's neck. She felt the blade bend against the floor and forced herself to look for the next blow and the next, slamming that blade into Issa's throat again and again until the woman had no more pleas, and her gurgling screams faded.

She didn't drop the blade or stop the hammering until the wet slap of her fist colliding with frayed meat, and Tobin's ever-present wails, were all that filled the room.

Now...

"You're not here. You're fucking dead." Shiv shut her eyes, refusing to see the corpse leaning into her, but she couldn't ignore its breath, icy and stinking of earth and decay.

"Yeah, not so much."

"How?"

"Some kind of magic. Don't know. I'm dead, not a witch. You *murdered* me, not sent me to Hogwarts."

"That's not possible." Shiv opened her eyes, and dammit if she wasn't arguing with a dead woman. This was no hallucination. "You're dead. You fell. You died. It's not m'fault. You were already dead."

Issa shook her head slowly, the movement creating little ticking sounds with the grinding of poorly aligned vertebrae.

"*You* did this," Issa said, poking a sinewy fingertip to Shiv's forehead accusingly. "This is me now. I'm a rotting corpse. An empty, cold, rotten corpse."

Denial was on the tip of her tongue, but so was something cold and wriggling. She knew what it was before she slapped at her mouth, pawing ineffectively at the sticky larva that clung to her gums. She gagged, movement at the back of her throat setting off the reflex as much as knowing what was crawling up her throat and flooding her mouth. When she doubled over and vomited, it was a soup of chubby, milk-white maggots mixed with hunks of rotten meat. Not meat, but her insides. She was literally puking her guts up in great convulsing heaves, and she gagged and retched until she, too, felt cold and empty inside, her throat raw and bleeding.

"I loved you, Shiv. You didn't have to get rid of me, tell Joe I'd abandoned him. You didn't have to do it, Shiv. I would have forgiven you."

"I didn't want to hurt you. I never meant to hurt you. I was…scared."

"So…was I."

Shiv's pulse jumped with the first buzzing of a greenfly that whizzed past her nose. It was joined by another in short order—attracted, no doubt, to all the putrefied flesh and human rot Shiv was sitting in. The swarm came gradually, its buzz becoming a roar, the air dotted with fat flies like static clouding the air. Some landed in her hair or lighted on her face as if to check her out, but others dived into her crevices, her ears and nose, pushing at the corners of her lips, testing the ripeness of every moist crack for housing eggs.

Shiv smacked them away, but they persisted, biting, stinging, until she had to rub every inch of exposed flesh to chase away the itching and pain. Rivers of crimson flowed in the wake of digging nails, but even raking deep into the fascia of her arms and body couldn't soothe the itch.

The static grew louder, joined by a snapping and crackling like pop rock candy or rice cereal. Beneath the blood under her nails, bits of wriggly larvae clung. The stripped-away hide revealed rows and rows of tightly packed white dots, the heads or tails of living fibres that made up the carpet of maggots beneath her skin. They were consuming her from the inside, the layer of parasites tunnelling beneath the dermis and lifting it, sucking it dry of life and moisture until her skin hardened around them like a full-body scab.

The smell of decay filled the room: a sweet, pungent bile, rotting fruit, and decomposing carrion. But then the bulbous body of a fly, too large to be real, settled on her lip and pushed into her nostril. It stretched the cavity, warping her nose out of shape, refusing to be pried away as she dug her fingers into her face and ripped at the insect. The hard bristles of its body were barbs in her flesh. It pushed deeper, because she couldn't stop it, violating her face with its pulsating bulk until her ability to breathe through her nose was completely blocked.

Shiv cried out, head tipping back as an agonised moan erupted from her throat, the barest beginning of a plea, of Issa's name, and a desperate appeal for help cut off by a clod of putrid soil bubbling up from her throat.

"You're fine. Everything is fine." Issa took Shiv's face in her hands and pressed her dead lips to her lover's own, undeterred by the grave dirt that spilled around the woman's teeth to pile in her lap. Then she pulled back enough to take in Shiv's terrified eyes as a milky haze drained all colour from her irises. She had no comfort to give the woman, save for the only thing that had soothed her once, as insincere as that promise had been. "The baby's going to be fine. With me and Joe..."

The house was quiet when Joe made it in, which wasn't unusual—Shiv was likely in bed, and Tobin had no doubt cried himself to sleep. Fortunately, this would be the last long trip he would be making for a while. Tobin needed an involved parent, and Shiv...

Hell, he didn't know what Shiv needed.

He shrugged off his bag by the door and made his way down the hall quietly so as not to disturb anyone. For a heartbeat, his steps stalled by Shiv's bedroom door, and then he moved on, opting not to deal with *that* first thing if he didn't have to. Instead, he checked in on the baby, prepared to give him a change and a cuddle in some meagre effort to make up for leaving him effectively alone all week.

"I thought I heard you come in." Shiv sat with Tobin in the middle of the floor, a thick blanket laid out to separate them from the hardwood as the baby pushed square pegs against round holes of a colourful box. The baby was smiling, didn't look like he'd cried in some time, and Shiv…

She looked like someone had finally turned the light on. Her eyes were bright, that sourness no longer hung about her sharp features, and she too smiled up at him. He hadn't seen that smile since well before Tobin had arrived.

Without a second thought, he let his legs collapse under him and sat beside her. He was prepared for the turn, for the snark, the demands for an update on the work situation, which for once he was eager to give. He wasn't prepared for her to lean into him, wrapping an arm about his neck and pulling him in tight.

He wasn't prepared for that sweetly murmured, "I missed you."

CEDRIC

UNHINGED

by J.W. Garrett

Damn witches…

Sweat clung to his face, dripping down his neck, and his breath came in small pants of air. Their magic bound Cedric tight, unable to move or speak. Stuck in his human form, he narrowed his eyes, seething as he gazed at the ring of women surrounding him, reciting words that made no sense. Piper wouldn't do this to him. She wasn't a murderer. She wouldn't follow through. Would she?

From under the hood of her cloak, he caught a glimpse of her face. Her body shook. Was it from the force of the magic pulsing through her veins, or was she crying? For him. Their love was stronger than this. And meant to endure. Maybe there was still a way out… Until she listened to reason, he could hang on for them both. If only Piper would give them a chance.

The chanting voices swelled, louder and louder.

Cedric wanted to scream at her. Tell her to stop this madness before it was too late.

He wanted to rip her throat to shreds.

His chest tightened, and the world spun. He gasped. *Air...* The chorus thundered, pounding out an agonising rhythm in his head. She needed to end this. Now.

His eyes widened, found hers, and the breath eased from him.

Three years later...

Piper woke with a start, her heart racing. Sitting up, she stared into the inky blackness. The windows rattled in her one-hundred-year-old home, interrupting the rumbles of thunder and the battering rhythm of rain falling in heavy sheets. The smell of candle wax filled the air as the rest of her senses kicked in. *Oh, yeah... The power went out last night.*

At the time they'd bought this place, Piper had been excited, ecstatic even, over the opportunity to take the Massachusetts fixer-upper and make it their own, applying their loving touch to the ageing monstrosity, as they turned it into a cosy home.

That version of their love, fresh and new, had been perfect, and they'd revelled in each second, delving deeper into their life together, blissfully unaware of the traps that lay in waiting in the not-too-distant future.

Dreams of that time often wove their way into her sleep, letting her unconscious work through the troubled thoughts that the light of day would not. Could there have been another way? Was her love not strong enough to find a path through? And if she had made the right decisions, why did the past continue to haunt her, causing her to relive those very same choices?

She groaned, scooting back under the covers, listening to the evidence of new leaks forming… *drip, drip, drip.* Tomorrow. She'd deal with it tomorrow. Beyond caring for now and lulled back into sleep by gusts of wind and lashing rain, her eyelids drooped shut.

Wind hit her face in tiny wisps of air, and a low moan echoed through the room. Through her sleep-addled brain, an eerie presence reached for her consciousness. No… She was dreaming again, right? A window must have broken during the storm…

The sheets ruffled, then drifted down again, her own body heat escaping in small waves of warmth. A shiver skittered up her spine, and she pulled the covers tighter around her, resettling deeper into the fluffy layers.

A light touch whispered over her shin, continuing

up, past her thigh and stomach, before tracing a slow circle around each breast. The touch was soft, achingly so at first, but the caress lingered, slowly cutting deeper into her skin, transforming into heavy groping strokes. Piper fought the intrusion, twisting and writhing away from the nightmare that wouldn't release her.

Icy fingers worked a path up her neck, patiently crawling towards her throat, stealing the air from her along the way. She gasped, reaching for the breath denied her. It wouldn't be long now; surely she'd wake. Because if she died in her sleep…well, she didn't want to wait to find out.

Sweat beaded on her forehead. A form took shape beside her. Thrashing, kicking, and flailing her arms and legs, she fought to connect with the thing that trapped her but met only air. The entity moved against her in an intimate manner she recognised. And even though she fought its influence, her body felt and craved the familiar embrace, betraying her.

It couldn't be… Her thoughts reached for the ancient tome, tucked away safely under lock and key, behind more presentable books. Was this still a dream? If so, none of this would matter. She'd wake and chalk up this delusion to the influence of the storm and her mind gone amok.

If not, Piper had an altogether new set of problems.

Years ago, she had promised herself to never again delve into magic or witchcraft. So she'd cast away the book of her ancestors—the one that had turned her into a killer. Well, that wasn't entirely true. In her heart, a part of her still loved him, but she needed him dead. For the public good, really. Plus, the two of them, as a couple, could never be, once she knew the truth, but the man was relentless.

She pulled upon a tendril of magic, wondering if those deeply buried paths would still be open to her, to engage, and to allow her entrance. The powers she'd shunned before, she called upon…now.

Her body roused from sleep, a tiny glow spread and grew, lighting up the space before her. Grasping the knot of light in one hand, she tossed back the covers. Nothing… No being, no object, nothing in the space with her that she could find. But along her legs and up the length of her body, dark splotches had already begun to form, the colour rising across her skin.

Definitely not a dream. Something or someone was in the room with her. Grateful her powers hadn't abandoned her, she took her search a step further. "*Illumine.*"

A shudder coursed through her when she spotted

him in the chair next to her bed. It couldn't be. How? She opened her mouth to yell, but only one word escaped. "Cedric?"

"That was fun." His low familiar chuckle slithered under her skin. "Watching you go from excited to scared to terrified in the space of a few minutes…and I'm so far from done."

Her eyes widened as she gazed at the man she'd killed years before, talking to her like he'd never left.

"Despite everything, you miss me. I could tell. Seemed like old times for a few minutes, except for the fact I'm dead and all."

"Right. Dead," she confirmed, glancing at herself, then sliding her gaze back to meet his. "So…"

"How am I here? Good question. Hell if I know. But I do have quite a few thoughts about what I'm gonna do, now that I'm getting this ghosting thing down." He stretched his arms and legs, then leaned in closer to her. "That's right. I'm a ghost, thanks to you. It's different here, than among all the other ghosts." A wicked grin crossed his face. "The living have a certain quality, a glistening almost. Makes you easy to find."

Piper swallowed hard.

He shrugged. "You killed me, and I loved you. We could have had everything…"

"I told you I could never be…what you were. You wouldn't listen."

"I guess I didn't. Love's funny that way. I would have done anything to keep you—then."

Scrambling backward on her knees, Piper increased the distance between them. Straightening, she got to her feet and turned to find Cedric right behind her.

"You don't get it. Do you? Let me spell it out for you. You can't hide from me. I'll find you. Anywhere…" Then he leaned closer, as he whispered into her ear, "For as long as I can, every minute that I can, I'll make your life a living hell, just like you did to me when you betrayed what we had."

"You can't. I won't let you!"

"What are you gonna do? Kill me again?"

"I…I don't know yet."

"Good plan." A smirk took his lips. "Can't wait to see how that works for you. Wait… Hold that thought. I've got an appointment to keep—one that you interrupted with your treachery."

Piper fought to steady her voice. "Stay away…"

"Only for a little while. Don't worry." The words left his mouth with the weight of a promise. "You see, these plans, they have to do with you too. So rest up, while you can."

Cedric's glee-filled smile seared its way into her thoughts, imprinting, leaving his mark there too. As her breath heaved and her heart thundered, his form dissipated. But his voice hung in the emptiness as he spoke once more. "I'm here. Always…"

Fear rippled through Piper's veins. Not the kind that seized a person all at once—the kind that slithered in, got comfortable, tainted the surroundings, then moved on to possess more of a life force, one beat at a time, before the prey even knew what gripped them.

Piper slid from her gown and dressed, wincing in pain, companion emotions of anger and embarrassment warring within her. Anger for Cedric's audacity, even as a ghost, and embarrassment that she'd actually hungered for his touch. She trembled as the visitation from last night replayed in her mind. Whatever it took, Piper would do to keep his ghost at bay, until a more final solution could be researched and implemented.

Her fingers twisted together. Opening that chapter in her life would alter her fundamentally. Last time, she'd almost not found her way back. *There's no other way…* Her moratorium on magic was officially over. The tome lay on the trunk beside her, where she'd placed it, after pulling it free from its hiding place.

Following Cedric's death, she'd sworn off witchcraft for good and had broken ties with her sisters in the craft. But the coven hadn't been hard to locate. In fact, Piper hadn't had to search far at all. Witches existed throughout her family tree. All Piper had to do was accept her path and pursue her gift. When she did, everything else fell into place.

She'd tried fighting her destiny, using her powers only when necessary. Somehow that made her feel less…evil. Now it seemed as if fate had knocked on her door, had handed her a verdict, settling the matter for her. Choice wasn't part of the equation any longer.

She transferred the grimoire to her lap, her hand resting on the pentagram scorched on the leather cover. Squeezing her eyes shut, Piper concentrated and let her thoughts guide her way through the tome. As she lifted the cover, the pages danced back and forth, mimicking her indecision.

Reaching deep within, she summoned the spirit of the coven to her, shoring up her will at the same time. The parchment stilled. Piper blinked, focusing on the word in bold on the page. Samhain… The festival would be about two weeks away now, in conjunction with the full moon. At that time, the barrier between worlds could be penetrated. Sounded like the perfect solution to her pesky ghost problem.

Piper devoured the words, page after page of rituals filling her thoughts. She'd need guidance to choose the best passageway for Cedric's unruly apparition. And a plan. Reuniting with her coven would lend her strength—a boost to her powers—which she desperately needed.

The summoning for the gathering took only seconds, and as she waited for the witches to arrive, she let her mind drift to her objective, but an old memory of Cedric came to mind instead—the dreadful day that had sealed their fates…

Another full moon rising in the night sky—another night without Cedric. But tonight she'd follow him. Get some answers. The explanations rambled around in her head. A clandestine encounter? An emergency meeting with co-workers, as he'd tried to convince her? Seemed like something more sinister… Soon she'd know the truth.

His travels led them deep into the woods. Branches smacked her in the face, cutting her skin, ripping her clothes, while hidden tree roots brought her to her knees, causing her to lose sight of him. More than once, she'd been certain he'd caught a glimpse of her, and she'd spent minutes cowering in fear, terrified of being discovered.

Cedric paused and canting his head, nosed the air, before returning his attention to his destination. A low growl filled the space between them, pulsating through the forest like a heartbeat. A shiver coursed through her body as she slowly followed his gaze, lifting her eyes upward towards the glow of the full moon that painted the skyscape in muted shades of orange and yellow.

As he fell into a crouch, inhuman sounds emanated from the man she thought she knew. Dread gripped her heart and squeezed her chest tight. The sight held her immobile and unable to drag her gaze away, Piper stared, unblinking, at the scene unfolding before her. Bones cracked, snapping apart, before reforming and coming together again into something new.

Cedric's spine shortened in a grisly fight for bones, muscle, and the remnants of what was once human flesh. Hands and feet transformed into paws that dug into the leaves and moist earth of the forest floor. Her blood ran cold, mere seconds ticking by, while the thing turned, raised his snout in the air and howled.

That night she'd stumbled her way back home in a mind-numbing haze, not sure what was reality and what was not.

"You neglected to mention you're a freaking werewolf. I saw it with my own eyes."

"And this is why."

"I can't unknow this now."

"You don't understand. Once I turn you, everything will make sense. This life… It'll be ours. Give us a chance. You'll see. You'll live for the hunt, just like I do. Right now, you can't feel it, but you could be alive like this too. I need to share this part of me with you."

"I will never want to be like you—one of those half-human animals…"

His eyes narrowed, darkening to murky black pools. "Don't say that," he hissed. "I'm not giving you up…ever. I'll die first."

From that day onward, Piper had delved into her heritage, learning all she possibly could about her ancestors hidden in the craft. Going forward again, she'd be one of them and would remain so.

A knock sounded. "Come in," Piper answered. Candles lit, herbs prepared and ready, the family grimoire at her side, she silently ticked off the list in her head. Time to get to work. "Ladies, I can't thank you enough for coming. I'm in this for good now. No turning back."

His unexpected appearance back in the world of the living had caught Cedric off guard too, to say the least. What he and Piper had between them wasn't over from his perspective—not by a long shot. But his death, and subsequent roaming through a purgatory of sorts, cast a veil over the hurt, but not lessening the ache that even the finality of his own extinction didn't quite conquer.

Stuck in his agony, he'd conceived a plan—how he'd kill Piper, if given the chance. Maybe this was the reason his soul had never fully crossed over into the afterlife.

Other restless souls found their way through the limbo of that awful pit full of suffering. How? Cedric never knew. They progressed onto another level of existence without his knowledge, while Cedric remained mired in the abyss of his pain. Maybe his return meant he should implement his plan, and, in doing so, Cedric would finally be free, and his restless soul would find a home.

In that vein of thought, Cedric arrived at the cabin, where his pack lived, when in a human form. And even though most everything else sucked about being a ghost, transportation with a thought was, hands down, *the* best way to travel. He chuckled. The guys were gonna shit bricks when they saw him, but it couldn't be helped. Cedric needed answers and living counterparts to lend action to his plan.

Hovering casually against the front door he'd just passed through, he waited. Utensils clattered against dishes, as the men shovelled food into their mouths at a steady pace, only pausing for the occasional grunt or slurp of drink.

The alpha, Jed, noticed him first and stood to his full height, his mouth falling open. "What the hell? Cedric? Is that you? *How* is it you?"

The other three swivelled, then got to their feet, matching expressions of horror covering their faces.

"Yeah, it's me. What's left of me anyway."

"But you're…dead. That witch of yours—"

"Look. I don't understand it all." Cedric shrugged and made his way towards the table. The four men took a collective step back. "Somehow the magical mojo went haywire, and here I am."

"Uh-huh… Guys, what the hell are we drinking?" Jed examined the inside of his cup and tossed it aside.

"I'm really here. Not a figment of your drunken imagination. So man-the-fuck-up and listen." Cedric took their silent stares as acknowledgement and continued. "Jed, it was your responsibility to finish the job. To turn Piper. She killed one of the pack. What the hell happened, man?"

Luke, Felix, and Earl waited to speak, gazes darting back and forth from their alpha to Cedric.

"Look. Give me a second here. I'm still wrapping my head around the fact that you're a ghost and standing right in front of us all. Let me think… Are you, uh, back to stay? One of us again?"

"I don't know how long I'll be here. If it's long enough to gain some satisfaction, maybe I can find some peace. That's all I want. Well, that and a few answers." The men's mouths gaped open, like fish flung from the water. "Come on…"

"All right." Jed exhaled a long sigh and ran a hand through his hair. "The shock's wearing off a bit. As I recall, by the time we arrived, the witches had already fried your ass. I called them off… What good would it have done to follow you then? The coven had the upper hand. Best to wait and attack later."

"And? Later? What did you do?"

"Cedric, my job is the protection and the survival of the pack. You know that. Since your death, we've all acquired new enemies. Ones we're still determining how to fight against and win. Our lives in exchange for your human didn't tally up in your favour. That's the bottom line."

"More important than honouring the wishes of your own brother?"

"Life is for the living. Simple as that. I'll bet in my position, you'd have done the same."

"Apparently I don't know you all as well as I thought I did, but in understanding the truth and what you know now, I need you to fix this."

Cedric waited, while his pack put their heads together, conferred, debated, then finally returned with a response.

"We agree. We'll do what we can."

"Okay. Now you're talking. Here's the plan to fix your screw up and exactly what I need from you. Don't let me down again, or I'll hunt your asses down… Yeah, that's right. Apparently I'm here for a while to do as I please. So do we understand each other?"

Empty stares and bobbing heads were his only reply.

"Good. Brothers, listen up."

The coven had guided Piper in various methods to keep Cedric's ghost at bay. Outfitted with salt and iron, at least one of her sisters attended Piper at all times. Their efforts relegated Cedric to the shadows, where he lurked just beyond their reach, until tonight. Tonight they'd rid him from her life for good.

Samhain still represented somewhat of a mystery to Piper, but she did know, during this time of year, the veil between the living and dead became almost transparent, allowing communion between the two. Her thoughts churned as the new summoning spells and rituals fought for space in her head.

Piper sensed the Horned God's presence, and—even more creepy than Cedric's ghost, since the coven had spoken this Horned God into their circle—the god's essence had been with her, inside her skin, waiting. The high priestess confirmed the incantation held the same effect for them all. Beyond the culmination of the spell, not much else made sense to her. Flipping through the grimoire, she read up on the Horned God and his gory deeds.

Years had passed since Piper had been to one of these festivals, and either she'd forgotten or never felt the call thrumming through her veins like this, pulling her into the fold, making her one with the forces of the night that now beat within her.

The sun hung low on the horizon, bathing the festivalgoers in dappled shades of light and dark. Fathers carried away sleeping children from the grounds, with wives following closely on their heels, blissfully unaware of the next phase of the celebration, as Piper had once been. With a flash of melancholy, she wished she could turn back the clock, return to the past, and make a different choice. But that wasn't her fate.

The coven and the life of a witch were.

And with the frivolity of the children's games over, the last young ones scurrying towards home, the mood of the gathered changed. Darkness fell, and hideously painted faces clad in ghoulish costumes took the places of the families who'd left. Piper ducked into the forest, down a path lit by candles secured inside hurricane lamps. After a short walk, the narrow trail opened to a glade.

The women beckoned Piper forward into their circle. She donned her cloak and flung the hood atop her head. And in a flash of vision, he appeared— Cedric—a predatory grin lifting his mouth. But the soul of another being concerned her more at that moment.

The coven swayed as they passed the potion between them and chanted.

The maiden, the mother, the crone...
The maiden, the mother, the crone...
The maiden, the mother, the crone...

Through stolen glimpses from beneath her hood, the coven leader raised the grimoire high, a spell leaving her lips. Thunder thrashed the sky, and lightning flashed jagged jolts among the congregated, but they continued on.

With their arms clasped, joining one to the other, their faces upturned to the elements, their bodies locked in a feral dance, time lost all meaning. Where was he—the Horned One—who took death as his companion? When would he appear? Sights and sounds blurred to a low hum; rain pelted Piper's cloak, seeping inside her clothing.

She followed her senses only through the steady rhythm pumping through her and the hands pulling on her wrists, perpetuating the group's circular movement, binding them all in their singular task.

Piper's mouth fell open as the scene before her stuttered into focus. The high priestess collapsed, and the monster inside her skin exploded into the crumbling circle of witches. His hide splattered in blood and bits of bone and ruined skin, the Horned God's gaze penetrated the ring, then focused on the blackness beyond, deeper into the woods. He leaned in and sniffed.

Yes, that's it. Piper pulled herself together. *That's where Cedric is.*

Growls and snarls echoed throughout the now-silent congregation, all eyes pinned on the beast and the ghost Cedric, marked to return to the Underworld with the Horned God before midnight, the end of Samhain.

Without warning, four large wolves burst from the tree line and leaped through the air. She glanced around her, the coven gone. Had they fled with the Horned God across the divide? Piper spun around.

The smell of wet fur mixed with the scent of iron, filling her nostrils, and then the wolves were on her. Pain seized her as hot trails of warmth oozed down her neck. The next bite ripped into her thigh, another dug into her side.

A scream stuck in her throat, spilling out as a moan instead. Writhing in pain, her flesh tore, shredding past the first layer of her humanity. The transformation overtook her body, moulding her, breaking her bones, reforming her arms, legs, and spine through a chorus of agony, creating something altogether new. Something feral, white, and furry.

She sniffed the air, tilted her head, and took in the world from a changed perspective.

Danger…

Dead wolves littered the ground at her feet. Only her now…and *it.*

Her lip lifted in a snarl, her long canines bared and

prepared to strike. A horned shadow lingered over her, lengthening, growing. The thing sliced at her and missed. Seconds wrenched by, as Piper sprang from the ground and sailed through the air towards her prey, aiming for the jugular.

What seemed like an eternal night broke into the darkest of days. Cedric had roamed aimlessly, since it had happened. Hell, he didn't understand witchcraft. Maybe it wasn't over. Or maybe their spells could be reversed, maybe the carnage before him undone. But the cold, hard reality of the day had confirmed that his pack had died, following Cedric's orders.

That monster the witches had conjured had taken them all—somewhere. When the earth had split open and had swallowed his family, along with the giant monster with horns, time had stilled. But what came next…

Their spells must have gone wrong. Piper's blood congealed in the mud, surrounding the spot where he stood, among small pockets of bones, hair, and teeth, all pooled inside the crimson circle. They were hers. He could still smell her.

Cedric lapped at her ruined remains; this way he'd possess part of her, carrying her inside him. Always.

A small sliver of sunlight shone into his eyes, and lifting his snout, Cedric howled long and low. How had he returned in full living form? He'd wanted her dead. Even more had wanted her to suffer. Because if she experienced even a small portion of the pain that tore through his insides, so much the better. And finally, they'd be together again. In death.

But an outcome like this hadn't occurred to him.

Now only he was left—a lone wolf—without her. With no protection or support of a pack, his future determined by his ability to fight. Padding into the forest, Cedric took off at a run, following the scent of prey. He raced harder...

The hunt was all that mattered now.

And in that, death was never too far away.

He slumped to his haunches, exhaustion doing its job. Night had fallen, but under the silver light of the almost full moon, he spotted the fluff of white before it disappeared deeper into the clump of trees.

Fatigue and hunger gripped him, but Cedric moved, following the animal. Shuffling into a clearing, his hackles rose, a low snarl his only warning before a white flash soared through the air and dropped on his back.

Piper? Her ghost? A strong jaw clamped around his neck. *Teeth felt real enough…* Blood trickled from his wound, matting his fur in a slow trail to the forest floor. Muscle and tendons tore loose as the maw dug deeper, shredding his throat, draining Cedric's remaining energy. His legs gave way, and curling into a ball, he raised his snout then gazed at the moon, mewling low.

Cedric scented the air. He was alone…

But his wound leaked his essence—that was real. *Where was she?* His heart slowed, echoing in his ears, as he glanced at the growing circle of red surrounding him.

His body shuddered a sigh, as the night closed in on him, its darkness encompassing, biting, and cold. A puff of air escaped his throat, and his vision dimmed to small slices of light that slowly winked out.

True death… He willed himself free.

SARAH

FORBIDDEN FRUIT

by Kimberly Rei

"Happy anniversary, darling."

The woman, dark-haired and slight, hid her cringe behind a smile and clutched a leather-bound book a little closer. His eyes darkened, but his own smile held as he leaned in to kiss her. She braced herself against the rush of fermented elderberries and honey. Something else this time, too. Her beloved husband had an affinity for blending his own spirits in the hopes of finding the perfect concoction. What that would taste like, he couldn't say. This one was very potent. Her eyes watered from his breath and when his lips touched hers and his tongue dipped into her mouth, she swayed slightly.

Laughter spun around her as he tucked her hand into his arm. She shifted the book for a better grip.

"God's teeth, Sarah, must you drag that thing with you everywhere? It's making you a laughingstock."

A blush swept across her cheeks, but she remained silent. He would never understand her need to cling to this particular tome. In part, because she struggled to explain herself. She only knew that she couldn't bear to be without it. This night more than any other. Instead of fumbling through an answer, she let her own question take hold.

"Why must we always meet here, my heart? It is unseemly and…dusty."

He laughed again and threw out his free arm to take in the entire cemetery. "Do you not think it elegant and peaceful? Where else would we go this late? All the proper establishments are shuttered for the night and you won't step into the other sort. No, sweet Sarah, this is our tradition. And one must uphold tradition, mustn't one?"

He brought them to a halt before a granite tomb. The top was flat and polished from centuries of breeze blowing across the surface. The four sides were rough and pitted, those same centuries far less kind.

A glistening bottle caught the light of the full moon and tossed it about, playing with the crimson liquid. Apprehension stirred in Sarah's chest. She pulled gently at her hand, as if to free it.

"Let us go. I have an aching feeling about this place.

Please. Can we not just go home?"

He shook his head sadly but walked away. "If you do not care for my choice of celebration, then there shall be none at all."

❧

Trevor snapped awake, covered in sweat and tangled in sheets. He kicked himself free and stumbled to the bathroom. Cold water didn't do anything but give him chills. He'd been waking from this dream every night for a week, always sweating, always panicked.

The first night, it was if he were watching a film. He could see them both, a silent phantom witness. The first night, the dream lasted for less than a minute. He knew, because he'd jerked awake and looked at the clock. One minute since he'd last checked the time.

Each night after, the dream played out more and more, fed to him a few moments at a time until he dreaded going to sleep. Friday night, he tried to stay awake until dawn, thinking that would spare him. He fell asleep on the couch, falling to the floor when an overly enthusiastic TV host screamed about a sale on chamois cloths. The dream held so tight, the scent of fresh earth coated his living room.

A shower did nothing to drive the smell from his nose or ease the chill in his muscles. A childhood of random illnesses left Trevor vaguely paranoid about his health, so he called his incredibly patient doctor. It was almost enough to hear his even-toned diagnosis of the head cold making its way around. Almost. Directions to spend a few days in bed with fluids and a good book was better.

A sneeze sent him nearly running to the corner store for cough medicine, decongestant, and a mystery by the inimitable David Green.

Trevor's grandmother once said he'd been born beneath an unlucky star. She said it at his hospitable bed as he fought back a violent and unrelenting fever. Karma, she claimed. Something from a past life was riding his back and wouldn't let him go until he faced it. An eight-year-old boy couldn't understand the concept, but he did love his Granny and hung on her every word. His mother was horrified when Granny tied a rough pouch stuffed with basil around his neck and told him to keep it close. The fever stilled that night, falling to near normal ranges. But when Granny went back to the holler and his mother threw the charm in the trash, the heat roared back.

Trevor returned to his small apartment and crawled under a pile of blankets with soup, medications, the book, and his laptop. The simple trek out stole away the last of his energy, but a definite spike of fever reminded him of Granny and her pouches.

What was meant as a quick search turned into an adventure down one rabbit hole of research after another. Mountain conjuring proved to be a fascinating exploration, revealing the reasons behind not only his Granny's oddness, but the relationship with her daughter. Trevor's mother was a true believer, Christian to the core. Granny saw the Bible as a grand story and a near-perfect spell book. Two sides of the same coin, neither able to see each other, planted back to back as they were.

He considered fetching some basil from the kitchen. It had helped once before. But no. Basil was for ghosts, and Trevor didn't have ghosts. He had a cold. His adult self smiled at childhood memories and drifted off to a nap.

🕊

They were fighting again. Thomas, she called him, crying delicately into a handkerchief. He tipped a bottle, swallowing the questionable contents. He paused in his berating of her to make a mental note: mistletoe and peaches made a terrible brew. Possibly even poisonous.

"Sarah, you will cease this nonsense. Reading has put uncomfortable notions into your head, and this women's group of yours is a waste of time. Why, you didn't have my slippers when I came home tonight!"

He allowed his indignation to paint his tone as he lifted a book from a small table.

"You will cease immediately." He threw the book into the pleasantly crackling fire, smiling at the dancing sparks and her yelp of denial. He caught her around the waist, preventing her from rescuing her treasure. His lips found hers, taking what belonged to him. She would learn her place and be grateful to him.

Trevor jolted awake, tasting dirt. A glance at the clock backed up what the darkness at his window told him. He'd been out for hours. He licked his lips and winced. The dream clung to him with a clarity stronger than the others. His mind was tormented, but his body wanted him to go back to sleep. Back to the dream. Back to what happened next. Not a chance.

Every corner of his home held ominous shadows and paranoia climbed higher. A cloak had settled over his shoulders, weighing him down with a story not his own. He was still there, still seeing Sarah's eyes as the man, Thomas, destroyed her joy.

Trevor sneezed, cursed, and stumbled to the kitchen to make tea. He stopped in the doorway, staring at a space that was not his own. Gone were all the modern appliances he'd spent so much care picking out. Instead, the heart of the house looked like something from the turn of the century. A few blinks and everything was right again.

Tea forgotten, he did a little quick math and decided it wasn't too late. She had stern rules about such things, but he was certain she would understand once she heard him out.

"O hyanh, boy. Whatcha want this time ah night?"

Granny didn't have a mobile phone, didn't have caller ID. She always knew it was him. She probably knew why he was calling but would wait for him to tell her. And so he did. The dreams, how relentless they were, how they carried over into his day. The strangeness of his hallucinations. The lingering sensation of not being connected to himself. The unbearable, unfathomable guilt he felt every time he woke. By the end, he felt better for saying it all out loud.

She snorted, "Ye throw the grounds?"

There was little his mother allowed Granny to teach him, but she'd managed a few traditions. Learning to drink coffee at eight made for a high energy existence, but learning to read the grounds had been terrifying. They were all too accurate. He'd been gone so long, he hadn't even considered it.

"S'what I thought. Go brew you some while I tell ye about Bert's cows."

She rambled all the local gossip (Bert's cows had got loose and wandered all over the holler) while he dutifully brewed coffee. Ignoring the heat, he carefully drank most of the cup, then stared at the last sip. Granny fell silent, leaving him to the ritual, as if she were standing over his shoulder watching him. He scooped a teaspoon of fresh grounds into the remaining coffee and leaned down to breathe into the cup. Once. Twice. After the third breath, he covered the top with the saucer.

His memories slid backwards in time to Granny's kitchen and the buzz from the rich drink. Granny didn't care for cream or sugar. As he passed the cup and saucer over his head three times, he could smell her biscuits baking.

"Keep yer mind on the task, boy. My catheads got nothin' to do with this."

He flipped the cup onto the saucer, setting both on the table. The saucer was set aside, and he peered into the bottom of the cup. The gasp across the phone connection reinforced the dread in his gut.

"Boy, what have you got yerself into?"

"Nothin, Granny, I swear, I ain't!" Another wince. It

didn't take long to fall back on old habits.

"Ya see em, dontcha? That dog. The heart."

Trevor didn't respond. He didn't need to.

"Death and love, boy. Whatever ye got goin, ye need ta get out of it. Make peace. Make amends. Y'hear? I done told yer momma, but she ain't never listen. I'mma light a candle for ye. Say my prayers. Ye call me in four days. Now go back ta bed. I can smell yer fever from here."

And like that, she was gone. From the phone, from his head. But she stayed close enough that his dreams, if they stirred, left him alone.

That night and the next night were peaceful. Restful. His fever broke, and he managed to get reasonably caught up on both work and emails.

The third night, the scent of earth struck him before he fell asleep, snapping him fully alert. He wanted to call Granny again, but he knew she'd have nothing more for him. Not yet. Four days, she said.

🕊

Thomas leaned back in his favourite chair and crossed his legs. He glanced at his feet and nodded to himself. Sarah had been waiting with his slippers, warmed by the fire, when he came home. As it should be. His whisky had been set out. His wife wore a soft smile and a gown of pale blue. He liked the way it set off her eyes.

He returned his attention to his newspaper. *10,000 Lives Lost in Texas Storm, Railroad Officials Say, 700 Bodies Found!* The hurricane that swept away Galveston was a nightmare of ungodly proportions. It was also very far away and so of little interest. Tragedies like this simply didn't happen in Boston. It was a proper place to live. Snowstorms were civilised, hurricanes barbaric.

Sarah stood at the door quietly, hands folded in front of her. When he looked up, she bowed her head gently. "Dinner is served, my love."

Warmth flowed through him at the sight and sound of her. She was utterly perfect and absolutely his. He needed to schedule a dinner party soon. It was one of his greatest pleasures to show her off from time to time, to remind his friends and enemies of the depths of blessings in his life.

He watched his wife turn on a dainty shoe and make her way to the dining room. Thomas lingered in his private sitting room, savouring the moment. She was his, and he wasn't ever letting her go.

He spared another glance at the headline and smirked. Poor suckers.

Trevor laid his suitcase on the bed and collapsed

next to it with a heavy sigh of relief. It was his deepest hope that he would find decent rest in a room not his own. His first book tour had taught him that strange places actually helped him sleep. Most of his fellow authors complained of the opposite, but he loved the pristine, transitory nature of a high-end hotel.

He had deliberately left his laptop at home. His cell phone was turned off and tucked in the side of his travel case. He was on vacation, and he was going to enjoy it. He'd never been to Boston.

His night passed without incident and he woke refreshed, bouncing out of bed. He sang in the shower, hummed as he shaved, and he was practically wiggling as he ate breakfast and planned his day on the town. Faneuil Hall, a couple of hours at the JFK Presidential Library, and a stroll through Beacon Hill with a stop at Cabot House. His mother thrived on a questionable, wrong side of the sheets, familial connection to TJ Cabot, one of the wealthiest robber barons of his era. It never bothered her how he'd made his money. Just that he had it. In her mind, Cabot pulled her ancestry out of the holler and into respectability.

Trevor wasn't a photographer. He preferred to keep his memories in his mind. But he couldn't resist texting a few photos of the Cabot house, from the outside as no cameras were allowed inside, and sending them to his mother. First and foremost was the plaque declaring the house a historical landmark. She already knew, of course. She knew everything about this place. But the image would make her day, and for all her foibles, he did love her.

After paying his entrance fee, he stepped into a well-preserved mausoleum. No one had lived here since TJ and his wife. They'd had no children between them, only TJ's numerous illicit offspring. But such was his reputation and power that his home had immediately been declared sacred after his suicide.

There had been rumours of more than just one death. Stories sprang up of his wife and a lover. Of a murder-suicide. They were quickly squashed. More than a hundred years later, the Cabot estate would still sue the oxygen out of anyone who dared breathe a word of the scandal.

Trevor paused at the entrance to TJ's sitting room. A velvet rope prevented him from going in, but he could see a newspaper on a small table and an empty whisky glass. He half expected to see TJ himself stroll out and scold him for trespassing.

Trevor turned and came face to face with himself. He yelped, skittering back a step, before realising he was staring at an overly ornate mirror. The room filled the reflection, placing him in front of the leather chair beside the table. He swayed slightly, dizziness overwhelming him.

Thomas watched them from the cover of a night-cloaked oak tree. Every detail of the scene burned into his memory, searing him with agony. He'd followed her here, to this most sacred ground. This was theirs. Their anniversary place. How dare she?

Soft, full lips covered Sarah's mouth. The kiss was sweet. Deep, exploring, and claiming. Sarah nearly swooned. She whimpered, leaning into the caress. The kiss grew more fervent and Sarah's book fell from her hand as she wrapped arms around her lover.

"Delilah." The sound was a sigh. A plea. An affirmation of too many stolen nights and too many hidden secrets. It was met with a rich chuckle as Delilah dug her fingers into dark locks, pulling pins free until silken waves fell like curtains to brush the ground. Delilah twisted a hand into a demanding grip, and Sarah's knees buckled.

"Tsk, tsk, love. No one told you to kneel."

Delilah laid Sarah across the polished granite and slowly, methodically, pulled away the gown covering her slight figure. Sarah shivered, at first from the lick of midnight wind, and then from the heat of Delilah's mouth covering a nipple. Sarah arched, nails trying to claw at the stone. The scrape of a lace glove on her thigh pulled her legs apart and her hips lifted in invitation.

Clearly lost in each other, they didn't hear him step forward. They didn't hear the snap of a twig under his shoe. They didn't hear the snarl slip free from his lips. They didn't hear any of it.

Until it was too late. Finally, they heard the cocking of a pistol.

Delilah reared back and spun, one hand holding Sarah still.

Thomas might well have been a statue for all that he did not move. The muzzle held steady, centred on Delilah's chest.

She shook her head. "Thomas, no. This is not the answer."

A single tear slid down his cheek. "It is the only answer. You were mine!"

Sarah sat up, clutching her gown to her naked skin, hiding herself from her husband. "My love, please! You must understand! I never intended to hurt you. We didn't...we didn't know how to..."

Her pleading faltered as the muzzle shifted and she

stared into a dark circle that promised only death.

"Your love," he spat the word back at her. "Your love is a lie and you, sweet Sarah, are nothing more than a harlot."

He pulled the trigger.

No sound echoed through the cemetery. No sound had shattered the silence for centuries. As the bullet left the chamber, three people tangled in a long-forgotten drama faded to nothing. Three items remained, one for each. A crimson-glinting bottle resting on the tomb. A leather-bound journal in the damp grass, opened to sketches of the female form. And a pair of cream-coloured lace gloves, stained scarlet with specks of blood.

෫

A buzzing sound filled her ears. She shook her head, trying to dislodge the irritation. Tension crawled up her spine. She was home, just outside her bedroom. She didn't remember going home. The last thing she remembered was the cemetery. Thomas. A loud noise and pain. Delilah falling. Her hands tightened and she looked down. Her book was a solid touchstone. The rest of her felt unsettled. Disconnected.

Something was off about the house. The lights were too bright, and the style was different. As she wandered, she saw every door had been removed from the hinges and the entry was blocked off with a strange red rope. What had happened to her home? She looked to the stairs and found herself standing on the ground floor, staring at Thomas' study.

There was a man. He, too, looked wrong. She knew him. But she didn't. But…she did. How she hated him.

"No!"

Trevor backed away from the mirror, one hand held in front of him as if to ward off the scene echoing through his memory. Two women, shot. A hand pulling the trigger.

Trevor could taste the gun smoke. His hand was numb from the kick of the weapon, as if he had fired all three shots. Behind him in the mirror, a beautiful young woman with a hole in her chest, holding a book close.

"You took her from me. You took everything from me."

He shook his head. He didn't dare turn around. This wasn't happening. This couldn't be happening.

"It wasn't me! I swear, it wasn't me!" The desperation in his voice cracked, allowing guilt to leak out. It wasn't Trevor, no. Not this body, not this life. But it was him. The moment he saw her, he knew. Some part of his soul recognised her.

She tilted her head, watching him, a fog clearing to remind her how many times they had met like this. "It is always you."

His chest tightened with pain. He looked down and stared at his own hand clutching a pistol, stared at the crimson blooming across his white shirt. The same pistol from the dream, turned on himself in endless absolution. The small, feminine hand wrapped around his, ensuring he would aim true.

He looked up into her blue eyes, seeking forgiveness and perhaps pity. He found neither in the ancient gaze of Sarah, once so demure and now so full of rage. He understood, finally, what his Granny was trying to tell him. Love. Death. And karma. Four days, she said. He was supposed to call her. He was supposed to live to call her. As he crumpled to the floor, the scent of basil and graveyard dirt filled his senses.

🕊️

A year later, as the moon crested impossibly full, Sarah stepped through the tilted wrought-iron gates, leather-bound book clutched in her arms.

"Happy anniversary, darling." Trevor spoke his line perfectly. One must uphold tradition.

JEZZELLE

THE BOOTH

by M. Sydnor Jr.

"Did you get her number?" Jezzelle asked, her gaze flickering at the waitress as she walked away.

Marcel choked on his coffee. "What? No."

She rolled her eyes. "Anyways, my parents came by last night and had *the talk* with me."

"The talk?"

"They said that I'm getting older—that they're getting older and wanted to know when I'm gonna get married and, blah, blah, blah...they just want grandchildren, so they can spoil and show them off." She giggled.

He added a nervous chuckle and touched the front pocket of his jacket.

"Spent all night stressing over that and telling my roommate how they should've come to your house and asked you."

He did laugh at that.

"Well, that led to drinks, and that led to a late night, which led to this bitch of a headache this morning. So, you gonna tell me why you dragged me out of bed to this filthy restaurant or are you going to keep me in suspense?" She reached over and grabbed a piece of his blueberry muffin.

As he gained hold of his feelings, manned up, he inched his hand towards that pocket. Then the waitress returned. "Your coffee and muffin, ma'am. Anything else for you guys today?"

Marcel dropped his hand and scoffed, annoyed with the interruption. "No, that's it for now, thank you."

When the waitress left, hopefully for good, Jezzelle was already three bites into her blueberry muffin, humming and sighing as she chewed. As she enjoyed her meal, Marcel slickly reached into his pocket and pulled out the ring box, slipping it below the table, out of view.

With both hands, he rubbed the box, tapped his leg, and looked at this beautiful woman who he wanted to spend the rest of his life with. He was mad at himself for waiting as long as he had. But he never thought they'd last this long. Jezzelle was sweet, smart, funny, beautiful, everything he'd ever wanted, everything he'd ever needed. No, she was too good for him. Out of his league. Out of this world. An angel this woman was, and he just a simple human. This was how he saw Jezzelle. A perfect woman who could do no wrong.

When she'd finished off the muffin, she leaned back and exhaled as if she'd eaten a four-course meal.

He smiled at that. *Goofball.*

No better time than the present. He lifted his hand to the table, box present, as she skipped the coffee for the glass of water.

"Jezzy?"

She set the glass down, looked into his eyes, then looked down at his hands. He saw her curiosity sparking, rising, then the front doors of the restaurant pushed opened with shouting men.

"Everybody hands up!"

Marcel looked behind him to the front, where four heavily armed men stormed the place. Two went straight for the counter, one to the left side, and the other one headed their way.

He was slow to hide the box.

"Hey you!" the large man roared. "Hands on the table."

Marcel ignored him and looked at Jezzelle. She was scared, shaking, eyes filling with water, and he was, well, scared too, but he wasn't going to show his hands. No way.

The table darkened. The smell of alcohol clouded the booth. The threat of violence was inevitable. Still, he wasn't going to give up the box. Then, he felt the barrel of the gun press against the side of his head. He turned his eyes to the man but didn't move. Not yet.

"I'm only going to tell you one more time. Hands on the—"

Marcel left the box in his lap, jumped from the booth and grabbed the gun, pushing it away from his head. A shot went off and tore through the glass window. The man was twice the size of Marcel, but not as strong as he looked. They were evenly matched as they struggled for control of the weapon. Another shot went off somewhere. Then Marcel kneed the man in his balls, which gave him full control of the weapon. The man dropped and Marcel immediately shot him in the chest. He turned to the rest of the diner and the other men scattered out. Was it him or the sounds of police sirens nearby?

He looked down at the man he'd just shot, red colouring on his white shirt. Marcel dropped the gun, turned around, and looked for the box, wherever it landed when it fell from his lap. He found it under the table, between Jezzelle's legs. Relief hit him as he returned to his seat with it safely in his hands.

Is it the right time to do this? Probably not. But he wanted her to know how serious he was about them. Their future. *This'll be a story to tell the kids.*

Finally, he looked over to Jezzelle and saw her head tilted back. Her neck stretched.

"Babe?"

No answer.

"Jezzelle?" He touched her hand. Shook it. Nothing.

Then, he jumped up and scrambled over to her side, and saw a hole in the centre of her face. Blood dripping out the back of her head, dripping onto the seats of the neighbouring booth. The life in him left, too, as he collapsed into her side of the booth, grabbed her shoulders, and pulled her head into his lap.

Sobbing and shaking and screaming…"Help! Someone help—"

"Sir?"

A blink of the eyes transitioned him back to the other side of the booth, and he looked up at the waitress.

"You okay, there?"

He felt weird, odd, but didn't know why, so he smiled. "I'm okay. Can I get a coffee and a blueberry muffin, please?"

"Sure thing, cutie," the waitress replied, then winked.

He shook off the strange feeling—thank the waitress' wink for that. She was gorgeous, he couldn't deny, but he was a taken man. In love. Hoping to make it official, forever. He rubbed his jacket, and the pocket over his chest, feeling for *it*. Made sure it was still there—it only made him more anxious.

Soon after, the waitress returned with the coffee and muffin.

"Thank you," he said.

"You're welcome," the waitress replied before bending over. "So—"

"Sorry, I'm late," Jezzelle's sweet voice came out of nowhere. He scooted towards the window, away from the aggressive waitress as his girlfriend took a seat across from him.

The waitress started to leave, but Marcel stopped her. "Uh miss, can we get another coffee and muffin, please? Blueberry?" he asked Jezzelle to confirm. She nodded. "Blueberry," he smiled at the waitress who had turned her mood to professional now.

His girlfriend watched her walk away, then looked at him.

"Did you get her number?"

He choked on his coffee, almost spit it up. "What? No."

She rolled her eyes. "Anyways, my parents came by last night and had *the talk* with me."

"The talk?" he wondered. *Wait...what?*

"They said that I'm getting older—that they're getting older and wanted to know when I'm gonna get married and, blah, blah, blah...they just want grandchildren, so they can spoil and show them off." She giggled.

What is this?

"Spent all night stressing over that and telling my roommate how they should've come to your house and asked you."

Déjà vu?

"Well, that led to drinks, and that led to a late night—"

To a bitch of a headache this morning, he thought the words as she spoke them. He remembered.

"So, you gonna tell me why you dragged me out of bed to this filthy restaurant or are you going to keep me in suspense." She reached over and took a piece of his muffin.

The waitress returned. "Your coffee and muffin, ma'am. Anything else for you guys today?"

"No, that's it for now, thank you," Marcel replied, the words spilling out of his mouth as if he'd been programmed with auto-response.

With every word spoken, every action taken, he couldn't shake the strong sense of déjà vu. But strange enough, he couldn't see what happened next. Only remembered it as it happened. And before he knew it, armed men stormed the restaurant and one was headed their way.

In his hand, below the table, a ring box was clutched in his hand. He couldn't recall how it got there, but he knew he had to keep it hidden. All urges pointed to protecting it with his life, and in a flash, he and the armed man were wrestling over it. One gunshot, the window behind him exploded. Another gunshot went somewhere, then Marcel overpowered the weapon from the man and shot him dead. The others scattered out of the restaurant, some of the customers followed, most stayed hidden.

Felt like he was on autopilot, the way his body moved on its own. His hands shook, his body trembled as he screamed for freedom. Freedom to get control over his body, freedom to grab his girl and run away.

The box that he risked his life for ended up back in his hand, on the table, and he felt ready to present it to

Jezzelle.

Jezzelle?

He looked across the table and saw her head stretched back.

"Babe?" he called out. Then, recollected. The blood pouring out of her head. Parts of her brain on the neighbouring booth. Still, he jumped out of his chair and ran to her. Tried to wake her. Still on autopilot, but he probably would've reacted the same way. Holding her head in his lap, crying on the outside, shrieking on the inside.

Back to the other side of the booth he went. As if someone had hit the rewind button…as if he were part of some sick psychological game that he had no control of. It was weird at first, a dream became the cause he'd constructed after the next four, five times. But at the rate it was going, it became more likely an unnatural event. This memory. The worst thing that had ever happened to him on repeat. The attractive but aggressive waitress hitting on him, the girlfriend meeting him, telling him about how her parents wanted the same thing he wanted. The attempt to propose. The robbers storming the place, interrupting his moment, his life, causing his girlfriend's death. All of this happening like it was yesterday. This was more than déjà vu. This was evil at play. And all he could do was pray and hope for this nightmare to end soon. This hell. Then it dawned on him.

Gotta end it. Gotta end this nightmare. Killing myself is the only way.

The tenth or twelfth time, hell, could've been the fiftieth, he'd lost track. Instead of shooting the robber, he turned the gun on himself and pulled the trigger. He woke up in his room. Sat up sweating, panting, looking around to see if it worked. It did. A hammer of relief smacked him in the face, and he fell back into the pillow. Sighing, relaxed. So relaxed, he could fall asleep again. But he stopped himself from that, jumped out of bed, and got himself together.

He tried his best to forget about his dream—the nightmare, but it'd only been a year since it happened. Yet, his daily routine carried on. He went to work and kept his mouth shut, even avoided telling his therapist about the dream. Poor guy was just hoping that it was an anomaly and that it'd go away. Boy, was he wrong.

The next night. Same thing. A nightmarish recap of his last date. Third time through, it gave him the courage to end the dream with a self-inflicted gunshot to his own head. He woke up to reality, went to work, went to therapy, and dreamed.

Another week of the same thing. Since Jezzelle died, he hated life, reality… sleeping used to be his only escape. Now, he was afraid to fall asleep, didn't want to dream. Didn't want to keep killing himself the way he was, just to wake up to more misery. So, he decided to purchase a gun and visit the restaurant. The same booth on the same day. What better way to stop his suffering, for real, than to end it in the same place that started it all.

That Saturday morning in the same booth, he ordered coffee and a blueberry muffin. A different waitress waited on him, and only him. The waitress didn't hit on him, his girlfriend didn't sneak up behind him, and no one came storming in with guns. This was real life, and there was no ring in his jacket pocket, only a gun. With the same energy, though; hesitant to take it out, hesitant to make this life-changing—life-ending—decision, he chickened out. Decided to live another day and face the nightmare head on.

He welcomed it, determined to get some answers. Easily, he fell asleep, but the nightmare never came. Only a dream about fishing. He didn't wake up in a cold sweat. His heart kept at a strong, safe pace. And he felt more refreshed than he'd ever been. The next night, he dreamt about racing cars.

Marcel had to go elsewhere for answers. Therapy.

Minus the gun he'd brought to the restaurant, he told her everything. And it was a weight lifted from his shoulders. She encouraged him to visit the same restaurant again, on the Saturday, in the booth, ordering the same coffee and blueberry muffin. To do that for a couple of weeks and the nightmare would never come again.

It wasn't the answer he wanted, but it was something.

He followed her suggestion and visited the restaurant the following Saturday. And the next Saturday. And the next. And it became a habit for him. Inadvertently upholding this tradition for fifty years. Fifty.

Marcel never married, never had children, and recently lost his job. Not to mention, he was prisoner to this filthy restaurant.

Today is the day.

"Sir?"

He looked up and saw the waitress.

"You okay there?"

He nodded. Didn't say a word.

"Can I get you anything?"

"Um…no…just…water for now, please."

"Sure thing, hun." The waitress narrowed her eyes,

trying to peel his skin back and peer into his soul. He looked away and she left.

Moments later, she returned with a glass of water. "I'll be back to check on you in a bit," the sweet old lady said.

"Th—thank you," he responded after she'd already gone. He sat there, alone, looking across the booth at the empty spot where he'd lost—

"Sorry, I'm late," Jezzelle's sweet voice came out of nowhere. He swore he was hearing things until he saw her enter the booth and sit. He jumped up, banged his knee against the table, and backed into the corner of his side like a child.

What the fuck? What the fuck? "What the fuck?" he screamed. If everyone didn't turn and stare at him when he nearly overturned the table, they were staring now. He looked away from his dead girlfriend and saw the waitress return.

"Sir, you okay there?"

On the other side of the booth, his dead girlfriend still sat. He pointed there with his eyes. The waitress looked at the spot, then looked back at him. Shrugging almost, confused.

"I'm going to need you to calm down, sir. I can call someone if you like?"

"No, no. I'm fine." He returned to his seat, feet down, and calmer, but he was not fine. Not by a long shot.

"I'll bring you something, hun. Okay? On the house."

He nodded. "Fine. Fine, fine, fine."

"Coffee and a muffin sound good? Blueberry?"

"No! I'll—I'll just keep the water, ma'am. Thank you."

"Eh, suit yourself." And she left again.

"You still come to this shithole?" Jezzelle asked.

He didn't speak, didn't respond. Just kept his eyes down and tried his best to ignore her.

"Marcel? Are you seriously going to fucking ignore me?"

You're not here. You're not here.

"Oh, motherfucker. I'm more here than I've ever been, thanks to you and whatever else it was that yanked me back here to find your pathetic ass."

Thanks to me? He didn't respond, but he couldn't stop the reaction of his thoughts.

"Here. I'll show you." She snapped her fingers.

"Everybody hands up!" the armed men yelled as they entered the restaurant.

The most damaging thing in his life happened to him again, as if it were the first time—the struggle; killing the man; holding Jezzelle's lifeless body in his arms.

And again, he lived through it.

And again…

And again…

And again…

These were more vivid than the nightmares that started it all.

"Stop!" he screamed. Then slapped his hands over his head. "Make it stop. Make it stop. Make it stop."

Whispers erupted around him. He peeked over and saw the old lady on the phone, staring at him. No doubt, she was probably calling the cops. He understood, he was acting like a crazy person. But he had a good reason for that. He was going fucking crazy.

He tried to get up to leave, but he couldn't move. Poor guy tried to push off the table, but there was no leverage, no movement. He was stuck to that booth. Some unforeseen energy strapping him down. Forcing him to face this, head on. He looked up and saw Jezzelle. Still as beautiful as the day he lost her. Tears streaming down his cheeks, he dropped his gaze. Couldn't stand the sight of her for more than two seconds. "Stop it, please?" he whispered.

"Stop what? I just want you to admit to what you did."

He never, out loud, admitted to what he'd done, even if he didn't pull the trigger. But he knew it was his fault. He should've just handed over the ring and she would've lived. Their bond was stronger than some material thing. But his pride, his ego, his little fucking piece of jewellery.

"I'm sorry," he said.

"Look at me!" she roared and the whole place shook.

He looked up, past her at first to see if anyone else noticed the rumbling room. Nothing.

He made eye contact with Jezzelle. "I'm sorry."

"Sorry for what?" she asked.

"I'm sorry you're dead."

She laughed. "You still don't get it, do you?" She raised her fingers to snap.

"No, no, no. I'm sorry I killed you. I'm sorry I killed you."

She lowered her hands and placed them on the table.

"Please. Not again. I can't live in that moment again," Marcel whined.

"Yet, you still come here. Every Saturday morning for the past fifty years. To the very goddamn booth where you killed me. Why?"

"I... I..."

He knew why—perhaps she did, too. But he wasn't ready to speak it out loud. He'd been putting it off for fifty years. But that morning was different, he was going to follow through with it. His life had been shit until that point. *That's why you're here.*

"Exactly. I know why. Just wanted to see if you had the balls to say it out loud. And you don't. After all these years, you're still a fucking wimp. If only you were man enough to propose to me beforehand, at the right time and location, I wouldn't be stuck here in this hell. You really think I'm going to let you kill yourself after what you did to me? You're not getting off that easy."

He reached into his coat pocket and pulled the gun out. Then placed it to his head. Someone must've seen him, because they screamed. Then another scream. Then everyone fled the restaurant, leaving him and his dead girlfriend alone.

"I'm sorry," he cried to Jezzelle. Weeping, he pulled the trigger.

The gun jammed.

She laughed, hysterically. "You silly motherfucker. You don't get to kill yourself. You don't get to take that away from me."

As he struggled to fix the gun, continuously pointing it to his head and squeezing, the table broke in half and the two sides of the booth split open. Like a volcano erupting, smoke blew from the hole and heat swarmed the area. Sweat overtook the tears on his face, and the gun fell in the hot hole, along with broken pieces of the booth.

"The only way I could move on was to take someone with me when it was their time. I've been stuck here for fifty years waiting for you to man up and follow through with something for once in your miserable fucking life. And, motherfucker, it's about to get a lot worse." Jezzelle's form started to glow as she hovered over the fiery hole. "You think me putting that tragic event in your head was torture? That was nothing compared to what I have in store for you down there. I'm going to rip your legs off and feed them to the hounds. I'm going to cut your arms off and shove them up your ass. I'm going to eat your heart out. Then, in your last breaths before you suffer an eternity of hell. I'm going to make you choke on that fucking ring box."

She grabbed his legs and dragged him into the hole. To hell. He screamed as his flesh burned off in his descent. He clawed at dirt and rocks, but he hardly had the strength and barely enough energy. He looked up and saw the ceiling of the restaurant, Earth, but the hole closed and that was the end for him.

"Hey, at least we'll be together forever now. It's what you wanted, right?"

CALEB

THE WILD HUNT

by Chris Bannor

The hotel mattress creaked as Aiden sank down into it, beer in one hand and the remote in the other. He wasn't interested in the television, but he hated the quiet. He had once revelled in the sound of the winds dancing through autumn leaves and the bubbling of the water over rocks and shallows. Now, he used old war movies to drown out the sound of voices that weren't there.

The glaring white of the bulb beside the bed hurt his eyes, but he didn't turn it off. Sleep pulled at him, but he wasn't ready yet. He wasn't drunk enough to forget the dreams come morning. The nightmares he would remember, but it was the dreams that always left him hollowed out.

Early spring in Indiana was beautiful, and he wished he knew why he'd returned. It'd been three years since

Caleb had died. Almost six since Ellie had. There was no reason to return to their hometown. He wouldn't visit their graves or reach out to loved ones. He had no one here for comfort and he didn't deserve it even if he did.

"What the hell am I doing, Caleb?" he asked aloud.

The television turned off and Aiden took a long pull from the bottle, trying to pretend it was just a mechanical error. Some sort of electric surge. He knew ghosts existed in the world, though. The supernatural might be legend and myth to humans, but he wasn't one of them. He might have shunned the sidhe and ran away from his people, but he was fae. He didn't fear ghosts, but there were some things worse than death.

He clicked the television back on and downed the rest of his beer. If he wanted more, he needed to run to the corner store, but he wasn't in the mood. Instead, he threw the bottle on the floor and listened to it clank against the others that had fallen there. He fell back onto the mattress and covered his eyes with his arm, content to pass out with his boots still on.

"Just leave me alone tonight, Caleb," he pleaded. "Just fucking leave me alone."

Grass tickled his feet as Aiden ran through the forest, fae laughter surrounding him as he raced further

and further. He was the fastest of them. He was wild and untamed, in love with the feel of the sun on his face and the cool of shadow under the trees. Some fae had learned to live among humans, but Aiden refused to be one of them. He would die in his woods, with his trees and memories to carry him to the Otherworld.

The laughter of others fell away as he outran them. He was at the edge of their territory, but he never cared for someone else's lines. He stopped at an unfamiliar river and danced the edge, following its trickling path until thirst called him. He swam to the deepest part and came up sputtering with laughter. The river was barely deep enough for him to swim in, but the water was invigorating, and he drank deeply of its cool current and allowed it to carry him downstream.

When he was properly refreshed, he laid back upon the rocky edge and let the mid-afternoon sun dry him as he napped. It was a light sleep, and he woke often to the sound of frogs singing and bumbles passing by in their dance. The third time he woke, there was a quiet around him that was unfamiliar. He knew something was wrong, and when he turned his head, he caught the eyes of a human woman.

"You're beautiful," she whispered in awe.

He pulled his glamour around him quickly, hiding

his true beauty from her. It was too late though, and he could see it in the way her body trembled, and her pupils dilated. He didn't speak. He backed away slowly, trying to keep the distance between them as she advanced.

"Ellie!" a voice called to her. She turned away from him to look, and Aidan used all the speed he had to leave the human behind.

He turned over in bed, head full of the past and heart beating faster than it should. He could feel something moving in the room around him. There was no sound, no motion that should alert him, but he could feel it all the same. The window was open, but it wasn't the crisp breeze that alerted him to something otherworldly in the air.

"I should have never come back here," he whispered into the darkness.

There was an answering pressure in his lungs, and he let out a deep breath to quell the feeling. He lied to himself that it was just a trick of the mind, but he knew better. He'd known for three years.

"Why do you have to haunt me? You chased me in life. Can't you leave me alone yet?"

Ellie returned to the forest every day. She was only

human, and there was no cure for the infatuation that occurred when a mortal looked upon one of the Fair Folk unmasked. If he hadn't strayed so far, he could have remained with his brethren, but she was relentless. "I'm leaving here," he told her as she chased him through the forest. "You won't see me again."

"I have to see you," she begged. She stopped running and fell to her knees. "I can't live without you. Why can't you let me love you?"

He watched her; glamour pulled around him so that he blended in with the background. He had resolved to stay this way. He had no other choice. Some people fell into deep melancholy and gave up on life, some continued on with the eternal sadness of seeing the ethereal and being unable to touch it, but some were relentless in their pursuit of it. Ellie wouldn't stop.

He heard the breaking of branches and he pulled further into the surrounding shadows. Ellie's brother came crashing through the underbrush and slid to his knees beside his sister. "Ellie, come home."

She pushed her brother away, and he landed on his ass in the dirt. "You don't understand, Caleb!"

"Just come home and you can explain it to me." He got up and offered his hand to her and she knocked it away.

"I'll find him, and I'll show him how much I love him. He'll realise he can only love me. No one else could love him like I do."

"Ellie, please, give this up."

She pushed him away again and rushed deeper into the woods. Aiden watched the brother as he stared after her. "Whatever he is, Ellie, you can't find him this way," he whispered. "Whatever he is, he isn't made to be caught by you."

The brother followed after her, and Aiden couldn't help but step out of the shadows to watch him go. He looked away quickly, aware of his precarious position, and fell back into the shadow. Until she left, he would not show himself to any other again.

The television turned off again; this time the lights in the room and outside his window flickered off as well. He sat up in bed and dropped his feet over the edge. "Her death wasn't my fault," he confessed to the night. "How can you blame me for yours? You tricked me. You came to me. You—" He stopped. He got out of bed and went to the brown paper bag that was always present on the table now. The beer was gone, but it was time for something harder. No matter where he went, the local liquor store was his best friend. He didn't know if a fae could become a drunk, but he was giving it his best.

He grabbed a bottle and didn't even check to see which one it was. He cracked the lid open and took a long pull from it, cheap whiskey burning his throat as he swallowed it down. Two more swigs and he felt calmer.

"If you're going to keep haunting me, you can at least let me see you again."

The woods had been peaceful. Two moons and he could finally show his face to the sun again. She had stopped her infernal chase. It was the best thing for her. Aiden felt guilt, but he hadn't meant to show himself. She would never get over her infatuation with him, but if she were strong enough, she could live with the memory of it. He hadn't thought her capable, but it had been two moons since she'd last come into the forest.

Aiden strolled the familiar paths and lifted his eyes to the canopy. The light green of spring had already begun to unfold—earlier this year than usual. He raised his hands to play in the shadows, dancing with the branches. He wasn't sure how long he'd been there, but the light had faded to twilight.

Aiden turned his head as he heard the crash of boots. He hid back in the shadows and under the cover of the trees. The brother—Caleb—fell to his knees in the middle

of the path, as if he knew Aiden was there. "You did this,"
he whispered. "You did something to her. Why? Why
couldn't you let her go?"

As Caleb punched the ground with his fist, there
was something beautifully tragic about him. He was full
of grief, but even with tears on his cheeks and anger in
his words, Aiden couldn't help but watch him. He was
graceful even in his violence, ethereal even in his
mortality.

"She didn't deserve to die for you. You wouldn't
even let her look at you. What are you?" Caleb screamed
into the twilight and Aiden wanted to give him some
comfort, but there was nothing he could do. "She killed
herself for you! You can at least face me!"

If he'd stayed with the fae, none of this would have
happened, but that moment had cemented too many
things in his mind. His guilt over his discovery had been
superficial at best, and when Caleb laid Ellie's death at his
feet, he had recoiled and ran. He had to know more,
though. He'd pulled his glamour around himself and
asked his brethren to take him to the modern world, to
find the truth himself.

Ellie committed suicide. She left a letter saying her
soul was crushed by a man who would never love her,

that she didn't have the heart to go on without him. The fae knew the truth, but they didn't blame him. They had no remorse for mortals. They lived their lives among them for fun, visited them for something different and exciting, but they hid among them, uncaring about the lives they might impact.

Aiden had tried to befriend Caleb, but the brother had somehow seen through it all. He knew who Aiden was, and it had set the path they travelled for years—Aiden always on the run and Caleb the hunter, never ceasing.

"Is this the payback?" he asked. "I hid from her, tried to keep her from following me. I did the best I could, Caleb. When she saw me, it was just a stupid accident. I shouldn't have been there. But there was nothing I could do once she saw me. I kept an eye on her when she visited the woods to make sure she was safe, but I never showed myself to her again. Only that last time, to tell her I was leaving. I hoped it would make her stop. I hoped she would look somewhere else. I didn't know... how could I know she'd take her life that way?"

He took another long swig from the bottle before he set it on the table. He sat in a chair that creaked too much to be stable, but he had grown used to it over the years. He never settled anyplace for long. Caleb never let him, not even after his death.

🕊

The job as a cook was a disaster and only his glamour kept the customers eating. He quit that almost as soon as he started, resigning himself to deli meals and fast food for the rest of his life. There were other sidhe around the country, but Aiden refused to ask for help. He'd always been too proud, too headstrong to go to others. Maybe if he had, he could have saved Ellie.

Construction was better work for him. Once he got on the team—and glamour usually allowed him to confuse them just enough to give him the job, even if they were about to decline—he worked hard and earned his place. He made good money at it, and it tired him enough that most nights he could sleep soundly.

Tonight, he was three beers into a six-pack when his phone chimed. Caleb was the only person who called him this late. He'd given the number to him years before when he thought Caleb hadn't recognised him. When he thought Caleb still saw him as human. Before Caleb had pulled a gun and shot him. He was fae. It hadn't hurt him, but Aiden had run again.

He never changed the number, and Caleb only called or texted when he was drunk or high. He grabbed his phone and let out a deep breath as he brought up the text.

Why can't I catch you either?

Aiden didn't want to die, but he was tired. He couldn't keep running. Three years of life on the road as Caleb chased him. Three years of Aiden wishing he could make Caleb see. Three years of sporadic conversation that made Aiden ache for something that might have been if everything had been different.

He typed the address of the motel into the phone and waited. He ran from Ellie all those years ago to try to save her. He thought he ran from Caleb to save himself. Somewhere along the line, he realised he wanted Caleb to chase him. He wanted to bring him home to the sidhe, to run along the wild paths and dance the river's edge and wait for a lover's embrace to hold him still and safe. He couldn't have that, but he was done running.

The power went out entirely and in the dark, Aiden saw the form take shape before him. "Caleb?"

The ghost gave off an eerie light in the darkness, but it was Caleb's delicate features that looked at him, sharp eyes that found him in the room and widened as if surprised.

"Caleb?" He stood and took two steps closer, then stopped.

"Aiden."

The voice wasn't quite right. It was too thin, too airy for the memories he had, but Aiden didn't care. Tears filled his eyes as he looked at the man he had grown to love. He tried to say something, but his throat was too thick.

"Aiden, you don't have to hide from me anymore," Caleb said softly.

The ghost came closer and touched his face. He felt no warmth from the touch, just cold against his cheek, but it felt more refreshing than any brook ever had. The glamour he had hidden behind for the past six years fell away, and he showed his true face to Caleb.

Caleb's eyes scanned his face, taking in the minute changes that made him more than human. There was none of the intense infatuation that plagued humans who looked upon the fae, though. Caleb was long past that now. "You are still beautiful, even when your tricks don't work on me," Caleb said with a small smile.

Aiden nearly sobbed, but he swallowed against it, forcing it down. "Why now, Caleb?" he asked. "Have you finally forgiven me?"

"I know I hurt you in life, but you have to know that in my heart, I never blamed you."

"Then why have you haunted me all these years?" Aiden asked.

Caleb's brow furrowed. "Aiden, I have been in darkness. I was dead and tonight, for some unknown reason, I saw the path before me and I came, hearing you call me."

"You weren't here before?"

Caleb shook his head. "If I could have seen you, do you think I would have stayed hidden?"

Aiden's eyes widened and behind Caleb, he saw the ghostly outline of another figure begin to take shape.

Aiden handed him a beer because he didn't know what else to do. There was nothing to say. When he heard the knock at the door, he opened it and stepped back, letting the man in. Aiden sat on the bed and Caleb dropped into the chair by the table. The motel was cleaner than most, but he was still embarrassed to have someone see him like this. It didn't matter that Caleb had followed him to worse dives. That Caleb's hunt had driven him to this lifestyle.

He looked down at his hands and found the words tripping from his tongue. "I lived in a world of magic. Everything was touched by it. The wind was a song and the earth spoke. It's too bad this is all you can see, this mortal version."

"There's nothing wrong with the mortal world."

Caleb was quiet as he spoke, almost defeated. "It might not be glorious or magnificent like your world, but surely even the fae can find something beautiful here."

Aiden let out a shuddered breath as he caught Caleb's eye. Their gaze held and there was a hunger in the other man that Aiden felt answered within him. "Yes," he said, but he wasn't sure what he was answering.

Caleb stood, then crossed the room. He towered over Aiden until he dropped to his knees to rest between Aiden's feet. When Caleb caught Aiden's face in his hands, he didn't try to pull away or protest. When Caleb brought their lips together in an unexpected kiss, he opened to him, pulling him closer.

"What the hell is that?" Caleb asked, even as he stood between Aiden and the thing forming in front of them.

"I thought it was you," Aiden whispered as a body slowly emerged from the ghostly fog.

"When have I ever hid from you?" Caleb demanded.

"Caleb? What are you doing here?"

The ghost took shape, and Aiden watched as the two ghosts confronted each other.

"Ellie?"

"Why do you have to follow him too? Once you left, he was finally mine."

"He was never yours, Ellie," Caleb told his sister.

Aiden stepped back, afraid in ways he'd never been. For three years, he thought the ghost of Caleb had haunted him for his death. The thought that it had been his sister, Ellie, was terrifying; that in her delirium, she had not only taken her life but also crossed the threshold of madness and remained a ghost in this world. That he'd confessed so many things, believing her to be Caleb.

"Were you always here?" he asked. "Was it always you?"

She looked past Caleb and to the fae that had enchanted her. "I wandered in darkness for a time, but then my brother's voice called out to me. That night, when he died, it pulled me to you. I understood then. Without Caleb to stop us, I could finally be what you needed."

Her eyes still pleaded, after all this time, and it broke something inside him to see it. "I never loved you, Ellie," he said. "You saw me by accident. You went mad from it. I tried my best to leave you to live a mortal life, but you chose death instead."

"And did you love him?" she demanded. "Did you love Caleb?"

He hesitated because the spirit before him was growing in power. Ellie had haunted him to desperation, but he had never felt the absolute malice that he felt now.

"He wasn't supposed to see you either!" she yelled. "What made him better than me? You spent years confessing to him! Why not me?"

Caleb turned to look at Aiden, but the look on his face was no longer the tortured soul he had once known. The pain of his conflicted truth had eased with death, and now he looked upon Aiden with clear eyes. And—it was enough to shatter his already broken heart—love.

"I left this place so you could move on, Caleb," Aiden said softly. "I haunted your heart in life, as much as you hunted me. I never wanted you to be left in this limbo."

"Don't speak to him! I'm the one you've been talking to all these years! I'm the one that listened!"

"Ellie," Caleb tried to speak with her, but she pushed through him and he dissipated instantly.

"Caleb?"

"He's already gone, but I'm still here, Aiden," Ellie said with a soft smile. "It was just us all these years. It can be again."

"Caleb?" he called for the man again, and in the corner, Caleb's ghost reappeared. Aiden let out a deep breath and closed his eyes. His knees felt weak when he realised the other man wasn't gone. He dropped into the chair behind him and looked back at Caleb to see his body form more completely.

"And still, you ignore me," Ellie accused.

Caleb came closer and Aiden would have dropped to his knees and begged for forgiveness if he felt he deserved it. Caleb smiled softly at him as if he understood. "I spent years chasing you. I would have spent a lifetime with you if I could, but fate was too cruel. You must know that I loved you though. Even without that face of yours, I fell in love with you."

Aiden closed his eyes, unworthy as he was of such words. "I loved you long before I admitted it, but I could never accept that you could love me as well. We can never know for certain now, but I wish it were true."

He felt the wave of malice strike just before he was thrown into the wall. Caleb, in his ghostly form, stayed as he was, unmolested by his sister's hate this time. "You killed me. You killed my brother. Now you want his love? And he's willing to give it? Who do you think you are? What sort of creature do you think deserves that level of devotion? We loved you, both of us, and you killed us both!"

"I never wanted to hurt you, Ellie. You took your own life. That was not my fault."

"And my brother?"

Aiden's voice was thick as he remembered that

night. "I would have died to save him. What happened between us…I can never atone for."

"That's right, you can't!" Ellie screamed. "I loved you so much that I gave my life for you, and I stayed here on Earth to be with you. For the last three years, I followed you and it was always Caleb you spoke to. Caleb you begged for forgiveness. Caleb doesn't deserve your love either! He betrayed me! He tried to keep me from you, and after I died, he kept you from finding me. From loving me!"

"Ellie, please you need to stop this," Caleb begged. "You need to let go and move on. You are hurting yourself, can't you see?"

"Shut up! You don't care about me! It was always about him! All those times you tried to keep me from going to the forest, it wasn't because you were afraid for me. You were afraid he'd finally see me!"

She struck out at the ghost again and Aiden tried to intercede, but she used a force he could not see to hold him back. He may be fae, but there was a power on the other side of the veil that fae magic did not touch. The fae were living creatures and had no power over the dead.

He watched them grapple together, two ghosts fighting with a force he could barely see, but he knew it wouldn't end well. Ellie was newly formed and furious in her delusions. Caleb was newly called, and with it had come a clarity that he had not known in life. If he had the same instability, perhaps he would stand a chance, but there wasn't enough rage to fight the sister he had so loved.

"Ellie!" Aiden screamed her name to get her attention. "I'll choose you!"

Both ghosts shimmered in that moment, and Aiden watched Caleb reform on the other side, while Ellie came closer to him.

"Choose me?" she asked. "Yes, you'll choose me, but you'll never love me, will you? I'm just the human you left to die while you played chase with my brother. I'm not blind to your games anymore, fae! I won't let you hurt anyone else again. Not me. And not my brother."

She stuck her hand into his body, ghostly fingers cold against the organs she penetrated. He gasped as a fist closed in around his heart. He might be long-lived, but the fae were as prone to death as any other creature. He felt his heart stop and the intense pain of it being pulled from his body. Muscle and tendon ripped, bone broke in her wake, until his bleeding dripping heart was in her ghostly hand.

He fell to his knees and onto his side, unable to

control his body anymore. Caleb screamed and he could only watch as she did the same with his ghostly form. The wisps of a green heart forming in her hand as she tore something from his form.

"Caleb," he tried to say, but blood splattered the ground instead.

Caleb's body dissipated, and he knew he wouldn't reform again. He would have wept if he had long enough to release the tears.

Ellie laughed over him, dropping both hearts to the ground. "I finally won your heart, Aiden. When your ghost forms, you will be mine," she said with the same wonder in her voice that she'd had in the living world. "This wild hunt is over."

His soul ached, but he had one comfort. He would not return as a ghost, bound by her in any way. He was fae. They had no ghosts. His death was final, and his heart, no matter whose hand it lay in, had already been given to the one he loved.

He woke to the feel of another body against his own and as he looked down, Caleb lay beside him. He felt the horror of the last three years ease from his shoulders as if Caleb had forgiven him for what had happened with his sister. As if last night had given them both the

permission to move past that tragedy and find a way forward together.

He was unworthy of love, and yet he found it here, in the most unlikely of places. After Ellie's death three years ago, Caleb had chased him. In the last year, there had been broken phone calls and shared regrets. They were both too tired to run any longer, too ready to give up this fight. Last night, they'd found something else entirely.

"Good morning," Aiden whispered as he trailed his fingers over the sun-kissed face of his lover. He traced the rays of light that fell across his cheek and studied the way the morning blessed his skin.

Caleb opened his eyes and smiled.

And Aiden felt the darkness slam into his heart. Caleb's eyes that had been so damn expressive, so fucking intense last night, were filled with enchantment. "No," he whispered as he pushed away. "No, not you, too."

But it was there. He thought back over the years to the look of obsessive hate and determined ruination and realised that the enchantment had always been there, buried beneath the violence of his sister's death and a need to reconcile his desire for the fae and his sister's obvious insanity because of him.

"When?" he begged. "When did you see me?"

Caleb looked confused, then seemed to understand. "I was there, looking for Ellie that day. I saw you, the same as she did."

Aiden stumbled out of bed and Caleb followed, confusion written so clearly on his face. "Aiden, I'm sorry. I tried. For three years I tried to hate you. I tried to hurt you, but I never could. I thought I owed it to my sister, but you were never hers. I know that. I couldn't stop following, though. I had to find a way to make you see."

"See what?"

"That you could love me," he whispered. "That all the ugliness you had seen in me, it wasn't who I was. When the darkness of the world filled me, it was your light that kept me sane. I needed you to know that it was love of you that drove me on."

Tears filled his eyes, and he tried to step away, but Caleb followed, grabbing his arms and holding him close.

"Caleb, stop. You know what this is. You saw it in your sister. Madness. Obsession. Enchantment."

"Devotion. Infatuation. Ecstasy. Or maybe, just love."

Words would never reach Caleb, he knew that. Once a human saw a fae without their glamour for protection, they remained enchanted for the rest of their *lives. He pulled away and this time Caleb didn't fight him. He pulled his pants on and sat on the edge of the bed to pull his shoes on. He reached for his shirt, but Caleb grabbed it and held it to his chest.*

"Am I supposed to let you get away so quickly?" he asked. "I finally got you to understand me, and you're just going to leave?"

Aiden closed his eyes, and he felt Caleb's hand across his naked shoulders. He shuddered under the touch, but he shook his head. "Caleb, I can't do this."

"You can't? You already did."

"I..."

"Tell me what is so wrong with this, Aiden?"

"I love you," he admitted. "I fell in love with a mortal, and all you will ever feel is the enchantment of my kind."

"I love you," Caleb said. He moved off the bed and onto the floor before him. In his hands was the knife he had carried throughout the years. The blade that his sister had used to kill herself. "I've hunted you for years, but this is yours now. This knife. This life. Whatever you want, I will give it to you."

Aiden got up and moved away, but Caleb caught him by the wrist and pulled. He was knocked onto the floor by his lover and Aiden struggled to get away. Caleb had the strength of those enchanted though, and it was no easy feat. He finally reached between them and pushed. Caleb flew into the wall across from him and Aiden was free. He scrambled to his feet and was determined to leave —shirt or none—when he realised Caleb hadn't moved.

He carefully crossed the room, ready to run the moment Caleb attacked again, but there was nothing. Aiden felt his pulse, and it was still there. He wasn't sure if there was something else wrong, but the wall had, at least, knocked him unconscious. Just out of reach was the knife he'd brought with him. The knife that had killed his sister.

The symbol of everything that made them so wrong together—even though just moments ago Aiden had believed he had finally found the one creature walking the earth who could love him.

He took the knife in hand and thought of ending his own life with the blade, but it would kill them both and he knew that. There was only one way to end the enchantment.

He held the knife tight in his hands and killed the man he loved.

Caleb would never love him. He would love no one because of the enchantment. This wasn't murder. It was mercy.

Even as he sobbed at his lover's death, he dropped the knife and walked away. He didn't deserve death. He deserved the misery of living with this crime. He deserved the pain of living alone through the centuries. He deserved to wonder, for all time, if Caleb could ever have genuinely loved him.

His hunger for his own demise was a wild thing, and he would spend eternity on that hunt.

AMANDA

THE MADNESS OF GUILT

by Crystal L. Kirkham

November 15

Here we go—my first entry in this thing. The doctor says that keeping a journal will help me recover from the pain of losing you. I think it's idiotic, but here we are. I've never been good or consistent with writing things like this, but I figured if I do it so that it feels like I am talking to you, then maybe it might work. I don't know how any of this will help me. My life ended with your death, and no amount of writing can change that fact.

Though, it feels nice to be able to talk to you. Pretending that you'll see these words and know how much you're missed. Although if I had my way, I would shut my mind off again, go back into that emptiness where time passed without notice. To that place where we still danced like we did on our wedding day. Forever and forever, into the darkness together, but you told me to wake up, and I did.

There are moments, every now and again, where I can smell your perfume, sometimes I swear I see your silhouette standing at the foot of my bed. I mentioned it once, but they say it's only wishful thinking: an overactive imagination spurred on by my "misplaced guilt." I think, as with many things, they are wrong. You are still here, watching over me. Maybe you couldn't cross over because your death was unnatural.

It wouldn't surprise me that a part of you still lingers here close to me. If it wasn't for that book. That cursed thing was supposed to bless us. Instead, it stole you away. I knew there'd be consequences, but this was a horribly cruel turn of events and it was all my fault. I will not deny that.

Time and time again, he's told me that my guilt over your death is misplaced, that I am not responsible, but we both know this isn't true. You told me not to dive into the occult, that it was dangerous. I didn't listen, and you paid the price. You were right. I should have left it all well enough alone. Amanda, I am so sorry. I wish I could take it all back, but I can't.

December 21

My dreams of you are becoming more frequent. Even after I wake, I swear you're still near—hanging about in the room. If I squint just right, I can almost see your smile in the ghostly figure standing at my bedside, but you melt away as the light fills my room, removing every trace of you from it. I curse the sun for daring to take you away from me all over again.

I don't tell the doctors or nurses about you being there anymore. I know they don't believe it's real. Last night, it was different. My dream wasn't of a memory or the pain of loss, it was of being reunited. Living on, not as if you had never been gone, but as if you had come back to me. It was so very real.

An idea sparked in my mind as you faded away again this morning. My life needs to return to normal, but I can't live without you. Obviously, I need to find a way to bring you back. If I can do that, then I can escape this hell that I find myself in. Perhaps it will even be like you were never gone from me.

It would be amazing to not have to carry this burden of guilt anymore, but the only question that remains is—how? I am sure that cursed book might have an answer, but what would be the cost this time?

I need you back, that much I know, and I cannot do it while rotting away under the close watch of doctors and nurses. Step one: Get out of here. Step two: Figure out how to bring you back to life. Step three: Live our happy ever after.

March 23

It took time—too much time—to get myself out of that place. Pretending to smile, to interact and be normal. Acting as though I wasn't dying inside every single day. And hiding this journal so that no one would accidentally find it and know what I was up to. I don't trust their promises that I would never be forced to reveal the contents of this book to anyone. Promises from those people are nothing. Not when they hold all the power.

Now, though, that isn't a worry. Instead, I am busy. Shitty job, shitty apartment, spending all my spare time researching. Your mom offered for me to stay with her, but I couldn't do that. It hurt too much to even think about having to look her in the eyes and pretend that everything would be okay.

She kept our stuff stored. She gave me anything that wasn't of sentimental value to her. I am okay with that. She deserves it more than I do. But she gave me back that book. I almost lost what little control I had when I saw it. The only thing that kept me from crawling my way back into the comforting darkness is the knowledge that I can't go back to that place if I want to fix what I did.

Not that any of this matters—except that book. That's the important part. I found so little information during my research. Lore and myth, all unfounded. Not a single valid ritual or anything. I even considered seeking out someone to help, but I'm scared to have to admit to another person what I'd done.

Eventually, I gave in and looked in that book. I read through page upon page of strange rituals until I found one that might work that wasn't too complicated. I tried it, and there you were. Your fingers reached for me as you faded away again.

I have hope. Hope that I might be able to bring you back. I'll keep searching. Eventually, I will find the solution.

June 8

So. Much. Research. If it wasn't so important to me, I would give up now, but you're too important. I need to make this work. I've been up most of the night, cleaning up from my latest attempt. Shattered glass, scrubbing the residue from the candles off the walls.

I wish I knew exactly what went wrong—was it

the ritual or the materials? Did I get something wrong in the incantation? Either way, the result was that I never even got to see you this time. It hurts my heart to write these words. I miss you with every fibre of my being.

I won't give up. I can't give up. I love you, Amanda.

November 3

For days I have avoided writing about the latest attempt. Every time I try, the memory of your screams rip through my soul and leave me a trembling, bawling mess. It doesn't help that ever since the…fifth? sixth? I don't know, but it was a few attempts ago; the nightmares have been getting worse.

I feel like I am failing you. No. I have failed you, Amanda. This last attempt…

This last attempt was the worst thing I have ever experienced. Like I was killing you all over again. I…I can't do this. I want to write about it, but even now I can barely see the page through my tears.

November 4

I couldn't even finish writing yesterday; the pain and memories of that last try took over, and I can't remember anything after that. I have to write it down, though. I don't know why, but it seems important for me to do this. Maybe it is just a habit now. I've been writing in a journal every week for almost a year now.

I can't keep putting this off. I have to write about the latest attempt. For a second, you were so close—almost real. There was a warmth in the room that I haven't felt since your death. I wanted to drop everything and run into your arms, to hold you again would have been the greatest joy.

And then, you screamed…

The memory of it hurts nearly as much as when it happened. Though, I should be thankful that memories don't make my ears and nose bleed. It felt like I was killing you all over again. Watching you shatter, disintegrate into a flash of bright light…and know it was my fault… I'm surprised I'm not back in the psych ward.

I need to find a solution soon and stop taking stupid chances. I can't risk hurting you like that again. I'd rather die myself. Hell, if my death could bring you back, then I would sacrifice my life readily.

I will find the answer, somehow.

December 24

Merry Christmas, Amanda. I wish I had something more to say. I've moved on from that cursed book. What mysteries remain in the rest of the pages I will never know. The night terrors that have been plaguing me since that one failed attempt would be enough to drive anyone insane. Night after night, I relive that moment; I relive your death, and the pain of every failed ritual.

Sometimes, I am myself, but more often I am you. The pain and anguish is near maddening. What I have put you through in life and in death is unimaginable. I wake up soaked from sweat and tears, my heart pounding as if it were trying to escape its mortal cage. It takes a few minutes for me to even realise where and who I am.

I've tried to avoid sleeping, but when I finally succumb to the exhaustion, the nightmares are worse than ever.

I can't even bear to face my family or yours this Christmas. I've received invitations from both. Instead, I have decided to stay here, in my apartment. I will not rest until I find an answer, a way to bring you back. I know I can do this. I must do this.

We both have suffered long enough. I need you. But, for the holidays, I will do my best to try to forget.

And if the only way to lose those memories is at the bottom of a bottle or ten, then so be it.

February 29

I can't believe how close I came this time. I couldn't even wait to write my entry. To feel your touch, to hear your voice—it was magical. If only it could have lasted forever, but that is the only part that hurts about this ritual. It was nearly the one. You were real for a moment. Here and alive.

Every failure, the nightmares, the suffering is all worth it to know that I have come this close to fixing the mistake I had made. Stupid Internet witch was sure there would be horrible consequences, but she's an idiot obviously. I am fine, you were alive, and the world didn't end.

I'm going to spend some time studying more on this latest ritual. I need to know how to make it last longer, to make it stable. Oh, Amanda, when you said my name I nearly started crying. Maybe I need more foetal blood, or perhaps it wasn't pure enough. I don't know. Whatever it was, I will find it and you will be mine. You will live and we will be happy again. I can't wait. I don't think I'll even sleep tonight. I'm so wired.

Soon, my darling love. Soon.

March 14

Failure. Every attempt since that one where you appeared has been horrible. I'm starting to wonder what sort of effect this dark magic is having on your soul. Last time…fuck. You weren't even you. The things you said, the way you acted. I let the candle burn out so that you would go away.

Have I made a mistake? Has all my hard work been nothing more than a pipe dream? My family and your family have both stopped talking to me. I've barely been able to keep this crappy apartment. Everything is falling apart, but none of that matters as much as the possibility that I have done more harm than good.

All I wanted was for us to be happy. To be together. My life has never been right without you in it. I just need to fix my wrongs and now… Are you perhaps angry that I have failed so much? Is that the reason for the nightmares and disturbances? For the dream where I woke up covered in bruises as if someone had been slapping and punching me all night?

I want to believe that it is only the result of bad magic. That with the right spell, I can fix it. I don't want you to be angry with me too. I need you, Amanda. You are all I have left now. Everyone else has abandoned me, but I need you to stay. I need you to believe in me. I need you.

I will fix this. I will make it right. There is no other option left. This is what I need to do.

May 1

Everything seems to be getting worse and worse. For a few minutes, I had you. In my arms, stroking your hair and then…it was as if a switch flipped inside of you. One moment you were the woman I loved and then you became a beast, a monster. I can barely see from one eye; the bruises and scratches are going to take time to heal.

To be honest, I thought that you were trying to kill me. Revenge? Madness from spending so long on the other side? Was it the ritual? So many unanswered questions.

Once again, I was forced to stop this ritual before it was finished. I don't know if completing it would have brought some sense to you, but it was clear you would have likely killed me before I had reached that point. It wasn't worth the risk.

I don't know what to do anymore. Giving up isn't something I think I can do. I need you so much, Amanda. I wish you were here—really here—to tell me what I need to do. I feel so lost and alone.

I don't know what else to do, but to keep trying. A part of my mind screams that this a mistake. That I need to give up. I'm not going to listen to it though because that would be admitting that I am a failure. And it means living with the fact that I killed you.

No matter what I must suffer, I am not willing to do that.

July 7

How appropriate that today is the day that I've decided to free us both. It's been two years since you died, and here I am, killing you again. The pain in my heart feels like a knife turning inside of me.

My body has become a patchwork of scars and bruises. Only a few of them are self-inflicted, the rest…the rest are from you. Your anger is a force greater than my will to bring you back. I don't know if this is my fault or not, but I would rather blame myself. Your death is mine and so is the destruction of your soul.

There are days where I cannot tell if I am awake or dreaming anymore. Everything blurs together. The seconds, the days, the weeks. I cannot even begin to tell you how many more times I've tried to bring you back, but it seems to only things worse.

I see your eyes constantly, but they are no longer the beautiful blue I fell in love with. Instead, they are lit with the red fires of anger and filled with a deep and bitter blackness. You are not you. You are gone and the creature that wears your face means to destroy me.

The only way to find my freedom now is to let you go. But it's not so easy as simply stopping my attempts a bringing you back. I think a part of you is stuck in this world, stuck to me. So, it's time for one last ritual.

If it doesn't work, there is only one solution…and I don't know if I'm willing to have another death on my hands.

July 24

Freedom comes at such a high price. I almost thought that I wasn't going to be able to do it, to send you out of this world and my life forever. I could barely move from exhaustion and pain for most of a week. I look like I fought my way out of a lion's cage. Maybe that's not too far from the truth.

Your rage, the ferocity with which you tried to stop me, it almost made me want to not go through with the ritual. To let you have what you wanted. I guess my self-preservation skills are stronger than I thought. I survived. I guess you could say I won—if you can call this winning.

That drawn-out wail as you were drawn back to wherever ghosts belong is something that will haunt me for a long time. It was as if I were tearing you apart piece by piece with my own hands. It took so long, and with each second you fought it. You tried to even drag me with you, I think.

It'll be a while before these bruises fade, and the gashes on my body become nothing more than scars in the same way that you will simply become another memory. My dreams have been different since that day. It's still you that haunts me, but not with the same soul-rendering terror I once felt. Guilt, yes, but I also feel free.

First time in a long time. Maybe the doctors were right. It's time to let you go.

February 15

It's been a long time since I've written in this. I'm not even sure why I kept this thing. I should have burned it, but I didn't. I've been doing so good over the last few months. No nightmares—until last night. You came back to me.

That same anger was in your eyes as you reached

for me. It seemed so real, and I awoke with my heart hammering hard within my chest. I hope it was just a dream, but I fear that might not be the case.

Please, let it be nothing more than a bad dream.

Garrett closed the worn, leather-bound book. He hadn't expected to discover much of use in its pages, but now he was wondering if this was truth behind the horrid murder scene that he'd been witness to. In all his years as a cop, he had never seen anything like it before. No doubt a few people were going to be seeing the department headshrinker for a few sessions. He was almost tempted to consider it himself.

His eyes drifted towards the pile of crime scene photos scattered on the table. Every gory detail captured for eternity in those images. It was one of those cases where nothing made sense. Doors and windows locked from the inside, no sign of entry and still, someone had torn this young woman to shreds.

A shudder ran down his spine as he considered everything he had read in that journal—she'd even written down the details of a few of the rituals she tried and notes on what she thought worked and didn't work. It was a bunch of nonsense but, at the same time, he hoped no one else ever got their hands on the information in it. Just the ingredient listed for some of them was enough to land a person in hot water.

Crazy and occult obsessed or not, that didn't change the fact that this girl was dead and, according to her notes, it may well have been a murder committed by someone who was already dead as well. He didn't believe in ghosts, but he was starting to wonder if this Kerri Nichols was a lot less crazy than reports made her out to be. Maybe—just maybe—there was something more going on here. It wasn't a thought he relished. "No, I don't believe in ghosts. Someone has to be responsible for her death."

As if in response, the lights flickered and an icy breeze ruffled his hair. Garrett shoved the journal back in the evidence bag, gathered the photos, and put everything away. No leads, no witnesses—he had nothing to go on. This one was going to be another cold case, and he was happy to let it stay that way.

SILAS

TOGETHER FOREVER

by K.T. Tate

Torn from burning joys, I'm dragged through unseen channels. Half-formed, confused, I emerge. For a moment I witness a strange congregation. Something stronger tugs at me, something familiar. The world blurs past me, sights and sounds merging as if underwater. Released into darkness, I pause. Familiar feelings start to surface. The echo of nerves and flesh, the inhabitation of a brain. Yet something is wrong.

Reincarnation? No, I don't think so. Is this my body? It can't be, I've been gone an eternity. A burning, glorious eternity. And yet it seems I'm back here, wallowing in the cold flesh and congealed black blood of my unbeating heart. I suppose time is a funny thing when you're dead. But what is the point of this? A new form of torture, perhaps? It *has* been a long time since I was on the receiving end.

Reality pools around me. All that I am sinks into my former fleshy cage. Instinctively I try to move, but it's futile. This lifeless shell has no steam. I tick zombie resurrection off my list. But what if…? I chuckle to myself. Of course. I'm looking at it wrong. This is what I once was, an anchor, a dead weight, but it isn't what I've become. No. The afterlife has made me what I always was inside. This must be a reward. A favour from the abyss for all my *good* work.

Instead of trying to open my flat, decaying human eyes, I open my spiritual ones. The ones that burn within my new form. The world comes to life. This shell, grey and transparent. The room almost 2D, a sepia painting. All the invisible things now shining smoke ghosts in my vision. One thing stands out most of all in the flatness. The reflective metal of the surgical lamp. It glimmers and ripples like liquid, a portal for my kind.

Setting my sights on this escape, I drag myself through the meat of man. Slithering out of the ichor, ascending, a small miasma of shadow and embers reaching towards the spirit light. I would relish in my freedom, but the mortal world that was once so alive now feels oppressive. It's as if I would dissipate if I lingered. The reflection welcomes me and I'm plunged into darkness. Void, awake with sensations I have no vocabulary for, pulls me this way and that. Like a deep-sea squid ebbing through murky depths.

A square of light twinkles in the distance. I force myself towards it, finding it to be a window to the waking world. A men's bathroom, to be precise. A tired-looking man stares at me but doesn't see me. Curious. His scrubs tell me I'm still in the hospital. I guess that my body was in their mortuary rather than a funeral home. Washing his hands makes it all click into place. Mirrors, reflections, they hide the void and its demons—me included.

Interesting… So, I can watch the world undetected? Joy fills me, sick and thick with longing. That means I can watch you, my darling. We can finally be together. But first I need to find you. If my body is fresh in the morgue, then you're probably still in the hospital. I wonder if dearest dad survived? Surely you're by his side. Did he tell you of his dirty little secret? No matter. Once we are together, I'll explain it all to you, my love.

Conjuring your image, I feel myself ripple. Nothing but a waveform, tuning to your frequency. A scent, an image, red petals illuminate the darkness. I follow their Euclidean trail through the dimensions unseen. Occasionally a soul sparks and flares, leaving the mortal coil. It's beautiful, but nothing compared to you. So beautiful, so delicate, like a flower. Blossoming roses fill my senses. I'm close.

A window, the mirror in his room shows me what I want. Nurses surround Harold as machines sing of his death. His soul sputters, sparking before they claim him. Tendrils drag him downwards. I'm unsurprised at his fate, considering he got into my debt. One day that will be a fond story. A funny story. A tale of how I found you, looking for leverage, for bait, and yet found the love of my life instead. It would have been a great romcom moment, if you hadn't killed me.

I nearly die again as you enter the room. Oh, to see you. Illuminated, angelic, even sensuous in your grief. The only thing that lights up this horrific flat grey world. You storm straight up to the bed and scream. Delicate knees hit the hospital floor as you crumple. You surprise me. A rare feat. I expected an aura filled with pain, loss, and longing. A wilting of your gentle beauty. But no. This isn't grief, not at all. This shines so much brighter.

This is anger.

Curious, I can't look away from this new you. You

don't see me, of course. You are more than a bit preoccupied. Using what little strength you have, you hoist yourself up. Gripping the bed frame white knuckled, you scowl at your father's visage, shaking. I didn't think that I could find you more alluring, but your fury is the most beautiful and raw thing I've ever witnessed. My passion for you blossoms anew somewhere in the ember cloud that is me. My little warrior queen.

So lost am I in these delectable and beguiling new sensations that I nearly miss all the commotion. You, delicate, tiny, and frail, spitting a cacophony of pain as you judge Harold guilty. Fists rain down bruises on his now concave chest. Realisation sweeping over you like the dawn that he can no longer hurt you. Triumph lights you up as you punch him in the face, his false teeth flying.

If I had known that dear old dad was a monster, I would have killed him sooner, rather than in self-defence. Would you have smiled as I dissected him? Would you take the knife from my hand and shared with him your pain? My sweet Iris, I see that there is so much more to you than I'd ever dreamed. We could be so much more. I have no idea how I will make this work, but I will. We will be together, my love. I'll show you the way.

You're sobbing, hard and heavy, as orderlies drag you away. Tears really do nothing to sully you. Scenes of torture ignite within me as their filthy hands dare to touch you. But it seems I am powerless here, trapped behind glass. Regardless, I will find a way to be with you. Whatever hollow empty space Harold carved into your soul is exactly where I want to make my home. So I do what I can. I follow you.

Your apartment is how I remember. The concrete stairs still stained with my blood. Only hours ago for you, but an eternity for me. I don't blame you. Having two grown men fighting in your house, guns, knives, blood on the carpet. I'm not surprised you pushed me. I'll forgive you, my sweet. You'll make it up to me. My embers burn brighter as the idea of how warms my core. Oh yes, the afterlife is a fantastic teacher.

The door handle's reflection lets me follow you inside. Collapsing onto the sofa, you let out another scream of frustration. And then the tears come. Heavy rains of sorrow and pain splash against the wooden floor. In this moment you are delicious. Something swells in me as the aura of your pain fills the room. By an unknown instinct I breathe it in, consuming this fog of various sorrows. It is glorious, a delicacy. The more

I take in, the stronger I feel. Knowledge and instincts of my new form awaken to me.

And you, my love. My delectable sweetheart, you now have the tiniest dot of a hole in your form. I'm not sure what it means, but I know I want it to grow. Perhaps if it was big enough, I could fill it? Become part of who you are? Rolling, sated with your pain, drooling over the idea of being inside you, I grin. A fiery crack in my shadow. Oh, to coil around your heart and feed from the source. To grow inside you till we are truly one.

🕊

Days pass, your life moving on under the loving gaze of my many watchful new eyes. A gift from you. Your outbursts giving me power, changing my form. But you've settled now, and I fear feeding may stop altogether. But one phone call changes all that. Summoned to his funeral, nothing could stop me from attending at your side. You were so angry after the call itself that I was sure the event would be a buffet. Don't worry my darling one, I won't feed on anyone else's emotions. I'm faithful.

Trepidation settles over me at the sight of the old wooden church. It wouldn't do to be struck down. But for you I go, my love, even if the light burns me away.

Luckily, there is nothing holy about this place. This building contains nothing but the sins and sorrows of man. Entering it defiantly, I taking up residence behind the shining surface of the cross. Harold's vacant body, nothing but an effigy for people to cry around. Your family tries to console you. Your eyes stare vacantly as you make quiet pleasantries. They don't know the truth, do they?

Standing to give your speech, hands trembling, I see what they cannot. Your aura of suppressed rage. Where is the girl I swooned over at the hospital? Where is that avenging angel? This won't do. Gathering up my being, I try to call to you, to breathe you in, to pull at your emotions. Moving to the confines of your earrings, I pull at your aura, consuming the sorrow in the hopes of bringing out the anger. Do it my love, do it. Tell them, show them how you feel. Let go…

It starts small but builds swiftly. Every tut, every cough, or downcast look just makes you braver. Silent tears turn to sobs, to shouts, to truth. Soon they are arguing their disapproval, but it is all music to me. No one wants to speak ill of the dead. But now questions are raised, arguments break out. Did Harold really do that? The hand of your mother stops everything as she strikes you. Storming out, waves of guilt separate your family like a scythe through souls.

Oh my beautiful love, that was perfect. Head on the steering wheel, you weep. Let me help you, let me take that pain away. Fattening, I start to drip from your earrings, coalescing like some dark leech upon your shoulder. Wiggling around confirms that I have some substance before I fall back unexpectedly into the shadows. A new place for me. Languidly, I check my prize. The hole in you is bigger now.

I watch over you as your routine slowly turns back to normal. Work interrupts our day and friends keep you buoyant. The nights are still mine. Your night terrors allowing for me to comfort you. To gently feed as you try to drown the visions out with alcohol. But I know it won't last. Not with all the help and support you are welcoming. Darcy suggesting her therapist is the last straw. These friends aren't good for you. Only I know what is best for you, my love. I'm the only one you need.

Their willingness to help you will be their downfall. One by one your friends check on you, and one by one I whisper into their aura. At first, I'm unsure that they can even hear me, but the shivers, the asking if there is a draft, the downward turn in conversation, all let me know that my presence is being felt. Even burning brightly draws their eye from time to time. My influence is subtle and difficult to enact, but it is worth it for you, my love. I would do anything for you.

It takes a while, but as if by magic all of your friends have the same idea. A night out on the town to cheer you up. What you need, my dear, is some fun. A drink, lots of drinks, enough to let out how you really feel. You're drinking anyway, so why not with friends? I don't even have to convince you. You do that all on your own. Yet another sign that you secretly want this. Prepared, we head out into the night.

As the evening starts to wind down, I set to work. Alcohol makes your friends susceptible to my influence. Flowing through the shadows, touching their auras, I push my will into them. My words ring in their minds as if it were their own thoughts. Soon enough you're at a club, downing shots and oversharing. The escalation of emotions plays brilliant hues upon your aura, I resist, but only just. Instead, I watch and wait, pushing here and there, all towards bad decisions.

It's on the way home that my beautiful terror is released once more. Alcohol fuels bravery. The idea is all your own and lights up your face with mischievous intent. Friends follow, curious and laughing.

Everything is in good fun. Until you reach the graveyard. Cautiously, they keep pace, trying to convince you to leave, asking what you're doing. Silence falls as you reach his headstone.

Morality breaks the spell of alcohol. Desecrating a grave is just too much. They don't understand you, what you've been through. The divide between your experiences opens like a chasm in your love for them. Betrayed you spit venom, getting more in return. Tempers flare as unforgivable words are spoken. When we are one, we will have vengeance, my love. I will help you hunt them, teach them the meaning of suffering. It will be my red gift to you.

You try to take out your fury on him. Only a stone marker where a monster once stood. Hands all scraped and knuckles bloody, leaving stains across his name. Alone in the dark, you laugh. They've left you. You even say yourself that you don't need them. Don't need anyone. But I'm still here. I sidle up to your aura, gentle with it, and whisper an idea. Watching you dance in the moonlight upon your father's grave, I take you in slowly. So beautiful, tiny and yet full of fury, powerful and yet broken. Empty and yet soon to be full.

Without family or friends in the way, finally, I start

to properly court you. Changing from a man to a ghost to whatever it is I came back as has been challenging. But with your love, I have grown. No longer an ember grub but a full-sized shadow, no longer a man but something more, something tainted by the other side. I shift my shadow form effortlessly. Navigating around you. I think you see me sometimes. You jump, turning to the edge of your vision. Blaming it on the meds is easier though.

Do you like the precious gifts I leave you? All designed to bring us closer together. The vodka no longer at the back of the cupboard. Enough to catch your eye, to drown your sorrows. The magazine open on the advert for sleeping pills. Such a comforting idea, sleep. Turning off your alarm so you can get some rest. The doctor hands you a prescription, adding your name to an already overfull waiting list. I hate seeing you like this, but I must do what is necessary. You'll understand soon.

Night time has become my favourite. Passed out, exhausted, and self-medicated, you are delicious. Shifting my form, I slither through the shadows. Sliding onto the bed, across the sheets, I extend myself towards your skin. Enjoying your warmth. It doesn't take much to stir your dreams, to bring up old memories, already nightmares. Carefully orchestrating your night terrors. Too much and you might expire from your depression. I don't want that; I need you wrathful, but also vulnerable and wanting to be loved. Wanting my love. I need you, to need me.

I put all my efforts into cultivating your emotional storm. Invisibly dissuading all chances of compassion and recovery. I keep you hanging on, teetering on the edge. Your aura is constantly fraying, letting me influence you more and more. Letting me get closer to you. Stoking your anger. As it shrinks, my excitement grows. You're close now. Almost perfect. Almost empty enough for me to fill.

Shattering glass sings a love song.

The shadows in the bathroom fill with my presence. You scream for it to stop, your medication thrown across the counter in defiance. Shards of mirror protrude from your fist. Blood pools, an offering as you plead for the pain to end. Begging your aura burns away. I sense other presences near, but you are mine and I won't let them have you. You have no idea how beautiful you are right now. Like a phoenix. Burning, dying, and yet to be reborn.

Wide-eyed, you look up to what remains of the

mirror. Tears stream down your face as you look past your reflection. Anticipation fills me. All I need is for you to invite me in. To welcome me. There is nothing I can do. You must ask of your own free will, a test of our love. I know you want me. That if I hadn't died, we would have been together. That you would have loved my life of blood and fun. Please, Iris, my love, please…

Help me.

The barrier between our worlds dissolves. Your aura falls like ash, scared soul cracking open like heaven's gates. Opening my many eyes, I look at you and for the first time, you truly see me. Staggering backwards, you fall, pushing yourself against the wall. Oozing out of the shadows, I pour like tar into a tall dark form. Screams stick in your throat, doing nothing but gurgle. Don't worry, my love, soon I will be able to comfort you, touch you, be you.

Kneeling down changes your screams to confusion. Turning my talon to a hand, I reach out, touching your cheek. See my love. I mean you no harm. Ah, but you can't hear me. Shifting, shadowy tendrils snake silently across the floor towards you. Like ink in water, I contaminate what little is left of your aura. Surrounding you, finally truly touching you, my promises and love resound sonorous through you. You recoil at first, but understanding blossoms.

This is our way. Possession. Residency in exchange for an end of suffering. To weaken until we can possess. I may have worn you down, taken everything good, and left you hollow inside, but I did it for us. I can refill you. Give you love, revenge, understanding, comfort. I will never hurt you. Never leave you. I will make a palace for you inside yourself where you can be my queen, have everything and anything you need. Even if you die, we will be bound. Let me feed your love starved soul.

Wearily you nod and that is enough. You squirm as the space between us ceases to exist, your aura now my blackness, your body now mine from inside to out. Permeating you, there is now only us. Together we are perfect. Your incendiary rage only fuels the atrocities I have planned in your name. I'll teach you how to like it. To revel in the bloodshed. It is all for you, my love, for your revenge on those that so wronged you. I'll lend you my strength. After all, love helps both partners grow, and you have done so much for me. There is no separating us now.

Together forever.

MEERA

BEHIND THE FAME

by D.J. Elton

The view was outstanding.

Crests of mountains and valleys, dotted with the scattered grand plan of life and labour. The occasional farm and its surroundings graced the perfect green carpet, complimenting the deep blue sky. Now and then a wafting cloud formation passed by—solid and puffy like the type of pillow Alexi most enjoyed—so transient, they came slowly and dispersed into the background.

"Why did you do it? With *her*? How can you hurt me like this?" Meera stood facing him, blocking the sun. All he could see was her lovely Latin face, seething with hot anger. Drops of pain, like a frenetic morse code, slipped between her eyes and mouth. Alexi could think of nothing to say. He could lie, deny, or boldly confess. However, none of these options formed suitable words in his brain. All he could think was how beautiful this woman was when she was like this. He wanted to kiss her, take her in his arms, and hold her tightly, but it was not to be. A sharp slap across his left cheek had him abruptly standing up. Meera was going to hit him again. He ducked and pushed her away. She turned and twisted, backing towards the small railing behind the seat on which they had been sitting five minutes ago.

"Meera." As he spoke, the moment slowed. His words softly reverberated around the canyon as love and annoyance internally jostled for his attention.

"I love you," Meera spat at him.

She threw back her head, stepped behind the seat, then dived—seemingly mechanically—backwards over the railing. Like an albatross in flight, her arms spanned broadly as if in a rehearsed gesture. She sailed down, down, down…leaving Alexi standing frozen near the seat, stunned by her final haughty expression and her scornful pout.

A searing pain hit his temples, and it was at least ten minutes before he could bring himself to engage with the world. Doing the sensible thing, he shuffled over near the railing and looked down. He could see nothing except rocks, huge boulders, and the flowing, cold, green river.

❧

…Three years later

Alexi sat on his new, pale blue couch listening to the sounds of the approaching garbage truck on the otherwise quiet and calm street where he lived. He'd put the last remnants of Meera's clothes into several large plastic bags and thrown them out—he couldn't bear to see them go anywhere else, even to a charity. As the truck stopped outside his apartment block, a swooshing noise reverberated up the chute, followed by the clunk of the automatic arm as it clutched at the remaining pieces of his dead wife's wardrobe, and they disappeared into a bog of crushed, foul-smelling rubbish.

Alexi returned to lie on his bed, seeking the comfort of rest and oblivion and the relief of having had some closure.

But it was not to be.

The shadow of Meera hovered several inches above his bedroom chair, grinning a smile that was both ominous and fascinating.

"Please go away!" Alexi pleaded. "We're done. Please."

"You should have given my clothes to charity,"

Meera whined. "Is that the best you could do?"

Desperately wishing to extricate himself from the intrusion, Alexi rolled over to face the window, ignoring her and hoping she would leave him in the peace he prays for.

There was a frost in the air, as the light of another cheerless Saturday tried to penetrate through the now eerily grey room. Bulging clouds lined up menacingly along the horizon, contrasting with the shafts of pale purple that split the sky.

He looked at the picture on the wall—himself as a young boy, sitting on the lap of his mother—and soft, silent tears pooled in his eyes as he remembered the simple comfort of that time.

Recalling the scheduled meeting with the medium, Madame Zahar, Alexi abandoned his attempt to rest and quickly showered, dressed in jeans and a white shirt, and threw down a lukewarm coffee.

As he was leaving the apartment, he was again drawn to the picture on the wall. But something was wrong. He looked closer, and the glass shattered and broke into small shards, and a dark red cross slowly appeared on the canvas.

She's doing this.

The sadness he felt at the beloved, ruined picture

was secondary to the rising tension in his gut. Meera was capable of anything. He needed to be cautious. She could be dangerous.

After a late breakfast in the downstairs café, Alexi passed people in the street from all walks of life—the casual, the well-dressed, the elderly, the couples, the singles.

As he walked, he reflected on his fifteen-year, childless marriage to the dancer, Meera Balaski, and felt a sharp stab in his heart as he recollected the initial happiness he'd felt—*they'd* felt. But the love and attraction had waned over the years and become an ugly, competitive, and moody liaison. Meera sought fame, craving all its glittery trimmings from a young age. Whilst he had been her *rock*—the man in the background who had thrust her forward—her agent and husband.

At least, that was how Alexi saw it.

Meera's lament

It's my chance to get back to him. I'm so ready for this.

Some unseen force has pulled me back from the timeless void, and I'm going to get Alexi back for all the pain he caused me. All the bad choices he made on my behalf. Leaving me so aimless, so bereft of life and all meaning.

I hate him.

He's going to feel my retribution. It's what he deserves. Even if he has to die.

Yet it began so sweetly, like a fairy tale…

Alexi lived near where I lived with my parents and brother. He knew my brother, Martin, as they together in a city café and was often popping in unannounced to our humble home.

I was young, only sixteen, but I knew this young man was intrigued and interested in me, although initially I tried my best to avoid him. I would catch him watching me practise my dance moves. He became my admiring audience, and it helped with my confidence. When I danced, Alexi made me feel so assured of my body, free with what it could do. He was my muse; I know it. In the early days, he was the one who brought out the very best in me. He used his entrepreneurial skills to get me work and get me known.

Then it was such a fast time, and throughout my twenties, so much happened so quickly. We married when I turned twenty-one and then travelled—first around England and Scotland, and then we were invited to Europe.

I had so many beautiful costumes—peacock colours, sea maidens, reds like fire.

Alexi kept my program very precise. He was so good at that. And I loved it all, and I loved my beautiful husband.

Then something changed.

It started to become a match of wills between us. I don't think he could tolerate my fame. He had always been the leader, the one in charge, but then I started to want more say in the life I was leading, in my dancing invitations. I started to complain about what I had to wear. I had new ideas, but Alexi was firm, almost rigid, about what I should wear and where I should dance. Even with whom I spent my time. He was very controlling, and of course, as I am an artist, I could not suffer this restrictiveness for too long. It felt almost as if he were stealing the creative juices from my heart. I began to think of him as my Svengali.

So, *I* suffered, and *he* suffered.

Then he was drinking more, and we would fight.

But it was no good—my work and my health both suffered. I declined, like a drooping flower. I was sad. Alone. Desperate.

Then he started seeing other women. All very discreetly at first, but then he became more careless, and as our marriage was floundering, we stayed longer in London. I was not working so much, even though I even went out seeking work without him. Alexi wasn't fulfilling his role as a husband, a lover, or even my agent.

It was horrible. I could have died there and then.

We had a terrible argument and said the most cruel, ugly things. I think I had already died a thousand deaths. I suffered so much. My heart was numb. It was absolute hell for both of us. Then Alexi suggested we take a two-week holiday in the mountains to try to save what little was left of our marriage. He said he would only drink two glasses of wine a day and I would attempt to be civil and not emotional—it was a hard task considering how ruined I felt, but we planned to do it.

We *were* doing it, right until we went up to the top of the mountain, and the accident happened.

It was an accident—I know that. I was being dramatic, but I know Alexi thinks he pushed me. Figuratively speaking, he did push me…too far.

So now he is feeling guilty, riddled with remorse,

and I feel a rage towards him that hasn't subsided.

If he had only let me have more freedom. Not so controlling. I hate him so much for that. I will continue to confront him about it until he realises his error.

Fair or foul. I do not care. He must apologise to me and acknowledge what he did.

❧

Alexi walked into the foyer of the old hotel. The art nouveau décor was still fine in its shabbiness. He spied a sign in black lettering on a pale pink background displaying the words, "Know Your Future" and the name Madame Z boldly placed in the lower right corner. He pressed the doorbell and twitches of anxiety shot across his chest.

Why am I doing this? Am I crazy? Or just really desperate? I hope no one saw me come in here.

All manner of reasons go through his head as to why he should leave and go home, or go for a stroll down to the promenade. But then he recalls his friend, Perry, and their conversation in the local club last year.

"You're not looking up to it, mate." Perry was shaking his head. "You need to get some kind of help for yourself. Meera's been gone for almost two years now."

It had been a painful yet necessary conversation

for Alexi.

"Nothing's moving forwards for me. I can't get cracking. It's awful. Some days I just want to go under." Alexi gritted his teeth, looking down, reluctant to face the pity and concern in Perry's eyes. "It's not as if we were really close anymore, Meera and I." Alexi threw his head into his hands. He was not usually so dramatic. "But I can't seem to work. I can't get on with it. I just can't…"

Perry could see it was hard for him to be having this conversation, timely as it was.

"I don't want to see a shrink," Alexi mumbled. "Don't need that." He groaned, raising his head, looking at Perry through imploring eyes. They had been friends for most of their lives, so this was also upsetting for his best mate. Perry reached into his back pocket and pulled out a crinkly brown wallet, removing a tightly inserted business card.

He nodded sombrely at Alexi. "Here"—he handed the card over—"go and see this woman. She might be able to help you. My daughter says she's spot on, and she would know." Perry winked.

Alexi stared at the card in the palm of his hand for a few minutes. "A gypsy?" He eyed Perry, screwing up his top lip, at once both curious *and* sceptical. "Are you serious?" He felt like giggling as it seemed too ridiculous. Way out of his comfort zone.

"Yeah, matey. She's good. Just do it." Then Perry's interest moved to the mixed martial arts program that had just come on the TV in the main lounge. "Check it out," he said as he disappeared into a surging male crowd vying for front-row viewing.

That had been almost six months ago, and Alexi was even more anxious now.

It had seemed like the time to act. He'd never seen himself as a procrastinator, nor someone who took advice from soothsayers, but the nocturnal visits of Meera were continuing to surprise, scare, and irritate him.

He knew he was being haunted.

He knocked on Madame Zahar's door, a young girl of about ten pulled it open and stared long and hard up at his face with pretty, alert eyes that reminded him of an elf.

"I'm Alexi. I have an appointment with…" She took his hand in her small sticky fingers, pulling him into a room smelling of spice, incense, and ashes. She sat him on a chair, one of several at a low round table covered in a bright purple velvet cloth. Two cups and a Chinese teapot sat neatly on a small bamboo tray.

"Sit down," ordered the girl, delivering the reticent lamb to his sacrifice, it seemed to Alexi.

Meera used to visit places like this, he recalled, but without him. To the unknowing, he appeared relaxed and assured, his armour in place, but he was terrified.

Alexi sat and waited as the girl watched him curiously. The woman was late. He tapped his fingers on the table. When she finally arrived, walking in a stately manner, he saw Madame Zahar had a kindly face, but sharp piercing eyes that he imagined could see straight through him. *I can't lie,* he thought.

She looked more Arabic than Romany, Alexi decided. She could have been anywhere between forty and seventy years old, such was her demeanour. It was hard to tell. She waved her hand at him as if she were the Queen Mother. He mumbled a, "Good morning." It made Alexi feel more at ease, almost comfortable; he had never been to a seer, sage, fortune teller, mage, witch, or the like before, so it was an entirely new experience. He could feel his solar plexus whirling and twirling. It seemed he was excited.

"I have a question." He spoke dryly, as if discussing a project plan. "I seem to be unable to, to…" Oddly, he felt strong emotion coursing through him as the words came out, and his mid-torso area continued to whirl and rumble of its own accord. It was hard to articulate anything.

"Have some tea, dear." Madame Zahar smiled sweetly, though her dark eyes bored into him. "I can see that you're suffering. It's understandable…it's your…predicament."

Alexi realigned his posture and held his chin up, tightening his grasp on the small teacup in his hand. He sniffed loudly, aware that more uninvited tears were starting to form in his pale-blue eyes.

There was a rustling sound in the room; curtains moved. Alexi shivered. Meera sat down across from him at the table, pale and serious. He tried to avoid looking at her. *Good God! What is she doing here?* Meera lifted her arm and gave a small wave—she seemed to be wrapped in a sheet and holding a small piece of glass. Alexi could see blood on her fingers.

Focus man, focus, he told himself sharply.

"You have a strong bind. An attachment to someone?" Madame Zahar spoke, breaking the silence.

Alexi gripped his empty cup, a tiny symbol of support in this strange space. He had an acute need to be elsewhere. This was so highly uncomfortable. What did she know, this ageless, small, Arabic woman sipping tea with him?

"I can't seem to get started on anything. I'm spending too much time alone. I feel like I've lost my old self. I can't work. Everything's on standstill." It was an effort to mention all these details, but it was a relief to have someone listen. Someone who seemed kind. *Well, she is being paid to listen and advise,* he thought cynically.

Meera rapped on the table. "Let's get started then, shall we?"

Horrified, Alexi's mouth fell open. "Madame. Do you *see* her?" His voice was a whisper which Madame Zahar either chose to ignore or did not hear.

"There's unfinished business?" she asked instead.

"Poor Alexi," cooed Meera. "Always so jealous of my success. My success, small and insignificant as it was, was your obsession. You made me famous. You did your job. You promoted me. You sold your product. But our marriage went cold."

It was painful to hear, but it was true. The icicles sitting in Alexi's belly seemed to be slowly shifting. He wished Meera would disappear forever, yet was also acutely aware of his own failing, his own greed, and base needs.

She's driving me crazy, he thought.

He sat back in his chair, his face aged, and riddled

with defeat. He peered at Madame Zahar cautiously, wondering how much of the exchange she could see or hear.

"Can you not *see* her?"

Madame Zahar, a blank expression on her face, shook her head absently and raised her palms.

"Can you *hear* her?" Alexi demanded.

Madame Zahar ignored his question and patted his hand in a kindly manner. "More tea?"

Alexi felt a window opening, like a light entering a ruined building. His gut felt less entangled, calmer. Strange and odd things were happening on another level.

A calibration was happening.

He whispered, "I am *so* sorry, Meera. So very sorry. I was wrong. I'm suffering for that dearly now. Please, please go. Leave me alone. Please."

"This isn't over," Meera's words—her tone was cold, menacing—cast a chilling shiver over Alexi. "That's not enough, you cowardly dick." Then she left..

Madame Zahar appear to lapse into a trance; she sat very still, eyes shut tight, hands clasped in her lap.

Ten minutes silently passed, and Alexi grew restless. He expected to hear the medium start snoring softly as her breath seemed to be getting louder, hypnotic even. She continued to sit upright as if propped, yet unconscious. He didn't want to say anything or even tap her arm. He was considering what to do next when the "elf" child appeared at his side.

"It's over now." It seemed to Alexi that she spoke as if announcing the end of the world. She gathered teacups onto a tray, and then holding out her small hand, cheekily asked, "Got your money, then?"

"Hmmph." Alexi was feeling mildly rebuked, unsure as to whether the session had been successful or not. He peeled two hundred-dollar notes into the child's sticky hand. She laid it on the table, tapped his chair a few times, and nodded upwards. Time to leave.

Alexi went down to the pier.

Walking was helpful as his legs and back felt tight after sitting overstretched in Madame Zahar's chair.

He was trying to work out whether his visit to her had been useful or not, as she hadn't given any advice or direction.

And then Meera had tuned up and taken over.

He felt grim and angry. He ground his teeth as he tried not to think of Meera, but it was impossible. She was ruining his mind. *What does she want? Why is she haunting me?* Madame Zahar had called it "unfinished business."

Unfinished business. What did it mean? How the hell could I finish the business?

He stood at the end of the pier with a small group of fishermen to either side, ignoring them but still glad of their presence. It seemed that Meera would keep turning up, uninvited, in her ghost form, and accuse him of terrible things. He knew she'd always been the jealous type. And he didn't want her turning up here. It was all too much—he thought he might go mad.

The midday ocean soaked into his erratic thoughts. Always a panacea. So calm. Today the wind was just right—soft and gently warm on his face. He felt tired but still wanted to think it all through—how to get rid of Meera; how to end the *unfinished business*.

He propped his wrap-around sunglasses high on his head and stared into the deep green water. Maybe it was time to seek out another relationship? Find a woman. He hadn't thought much about it until now. He'd had several discreet liaisons whilst going through the most difficult of times when Meera had been alive. Women were always seemed to be willing to be with him—it was as if they felt sorry he had to tolerate a life consumed by living with and being the manager of Meera Balaski, the famous dancer.

BLACK HARE PRESS

He actively tried not to think about Meera—which was ridiculously hard—and, instead, Meera's one-time personal assistant came to mind.

Jane...

Jane Morris. She'd be able to help. He would call her when he got home.

Jane had seen Alexi twice since his call before he'd asked her to spend the weekend at Mount Edithe.

She was excited and a little nervous as she absent-mindedly packed, throwing warm clothes with abandon into her tight little suitcase. It had been a hectic week, with a new client taking up a lot of her spare time—the excessive phone calls, demands for hard-to-find items for their upcoming debut. Jane, however, was well-connected and felt she had done a good enough job.

Now it was Friday.

She sat down with a post-lunch cup of tea, eyeing her text messages. There were two from Alexi. Both were short.

Thursday 10:00 p.m.: *Looking forward to the weekend.*

Friday 09:00 a.m.: *Poor sleep. Feeling like a train wreck. See you at 4.*

She thought about how much Alexi had changed since Meera's passing. Jane hadn't seen him since the funeral—that had been a drab, soulless affair.

Alexi hadn't looked at her even once. She'd assumed he must have been riddled with guilt. Their time together had been brief; several short, snatched encounters between shows when Meera had usually been having beauty treatments or visiting a private gym.

They had been thrown together due to the nature of her being Meera's personal assistant. It had been hard to refuse Alexi's insistent demands on her to grab an hour or two at a hotel, or even at her own flat, when Meera was absent. She had felt the heat rise in her chest and the pit of her stomach—Alexi was a strong, self-assured man, and she had readily fallen into his arms because he made her feel important and desired.

Alexi's sleep had become more disturbed over the few days since his visit to Madame Zahar. He hadn't felt Meera's presence in his apartment, nor at any other time, but he'd started having conversations with her in his head, which was even more disturbing.

"I suppose you're going to fall for her and go on a little dirty weekend?" It was three o'clock on Friday morning, and Alexi's dreams had been full of repugnant scenes of sex and death. He had been making love to a faceless corpse, and as his movements became more frantic, desperately needy, he had awoken feeling disorientated and in a hot, sticky sweat. Aware of his erection becoming more flaccid as his eyes opened, growing wider, accustoming to the light, Alexi groaned deeply.

Did someone mention Hell? he wondered as the feelings of shame and rage subsided. He wanted to get up, throw on his old dressing gown, and shuffle to the bathroom so he could take a shower and clean himself up—he felt unclean. But it was useless—he couldn't get himself up. He lay back down on the bed, lopsided, and half-covered with blankets, and waited for the early light of morning to start to edge through the curtains.

He thought of Jane and tried to focus on her face. She was confident and able, someone who was getting on well with her life. *No ghosts*, he thought sadly. He visualised his head on Jane's shoulder, wrapping her in his arms and holding her tightly. It helped. It gave him some focus as he went about his day. He was looking forward to seeing her in the late afternoon, looking forward to spending time in an uncomplicated, earthy, sensual way. He really needed it.

🕊

As Alexi and Jane sat having breakfast together, admiring the breathlessly picturesque view from their top floor suite at the Hotel Edithe, Jane broke the warm silence.

"I love this place."

Alexi smiled broadly when she spoke. "I haven't been here for a couple of years. I needed to come back," he confessed, looking down. "To move on." He dared not say Meera's name in case she appeared.

Jane rested her arm on Alexi's shoulder, gently stroking his neck. He pulled her hand to his lips, kissing it noisily.

"You're my good medicine, Jane." He sat her on his lap, undoing her thin housecoat, hands on skin, burying his face into her neck and shoulders. She smelled of lilac. "Such good medicine."

🕊

They spent most of the day exploring each other—two minds, two bodies. Gently and frantically coming together. Alexi could feel himself loosening up; felt much more relaxed. He felt more in control, stronger, and he loved how Jane was bringing that out in him.

With only a couple of hours until the sun went down, a long indulgent sunset graced the sky, reminding Alexi of his day with Jane, and the promise of many more to come. He felt happy. They showered and dressed, having planned to take a short walk together. He was keen to get outside and move his legs, even take a run.

They set out together using a narrowing path from the rear of the hotel that led up the mountain. The scenery was fresh and alive. Alexi knew he was starting to feel whole again. His inner workings were shifting, and there was hope on the horizon.

Jane called to him from behind.

"I think I need to go back and get my camera. It won't take long." Alexi felt a brief ripple of irritation.

Why didn't she think of this before now?

"Are you sure?" he sounded doubtful.

"Yes, yes. I could get some great shots in this light. I won't be long. Just keep going slowly or wait at the next fork for me." Jane had already started jumping back along the track.

Feeling miffed, Alexi continued walking ahead alone. Unexpectedly angered by Jane's retreat, he raced ahead faster. He could meet her at the top. He didn't want to dally. He didn't like waiting around for people. Besides, his body could do with a swift five-kilometre uphill run. He started scaling the mountain quite easily and reached the top sooner than anticipated.

The air felt cooler and still. There was no one else around. Except…

Except…

"How can you do this to me? Again?" It was Meera's voice, sharp and clear, speaking inside his head.

"Oh, for God's sake." Alexi stiffened. "Can you not just go? Just go away. Let me get on with my life." He could feel Meera's presence—a cool, bitter chill that made him shiver.

"I'm not ready to go."

"Why the hell not?"

"You need to own up to your despicable treatment of me, Alexi. I want to hear you say it out aloud that you're sorry. Go on, say it. You wronged me, Alexi. You pushed me so hard to make me famous. And you controlled me. Then you had affairs. That's what happened. Own up to it. SAY YOU'RE SORRY."

Alexi felt a rush of emotion like biting birds in his chest. Annoyance. He was irritated with himself, especially because he knew it to be true. All that Meera was saying was true. Yet he could not bring himself to concede and apologise to her.

His ego wouldn't allow it—he felt as if to do so, would kill him.

"Go away, Meera," he said aloud.

"Just apologise *and mean it.*" Her words were screamed in his head. She seethed with a poisonous air, full of bitterness and confusion. Meera's face, flashing into view, was contorted with rage. Alexi could feel sharp pins twisting and stabbing in his belly.

"No. I don't want you here. Haven't you tormented me enough?" He felt weary. So, so weary. This woman would do anything to get back at him, anything to make him suffer even more than she had, just to call him out. *She* had the control now, and he was *her* victim.

He shuddered as an iron fist clutched and squeezed his heart. His breath became shallow as the oxygen to his brain become sparser.

Will this ever end?

It occurred to him that he could do nothing. It was decreed, laid out. Destined.

Morose and defeated, he took in the view. The deep late afternoon sunlight was flashing through the trees, shining a subtle golden light and creating an almost-magical land.

It was so exhausting, all this battling of wits with a ghost. For God's sake. Would it never stop? She was relentless.

He looked back down the path but still couldn't see Jane anywhere. Maybe she hadn't come back up again. Oh well.

Then he felt Meera's thin, strong arms reaching out to him, pulling him into an embrace. She led him on a slow waltz around the level ground at the peak that he so loved, even with its dismal memories. Alexi succumbed to this unusual movement, although it was somewhat repulsive to him. He could see Meera's outline as she lay her head on his chest, directing the movement of this macabre dance.

He surrendered to it—what else could he do?

But then, in a quick movement, he jumped away from Meera's gripping arms and free-fell, ever so slowly. A soaring flight.

Just one thought held him. *I want all of this to stop.*

It was as if Meera had called him, shown him the way. *This* way. The only way to relieve his conscience, to relieve her pain, and his stubbornness was to die.

The wonder was that Alexi finally realised that, in his dying dive.

He'd enabled Meera in the karmic scheme of

things. *That* was what she'd so desperately wanted all along.

Alexi's death set Meera free. She would never return to accuse him. All was done, and her time had come to go forward.

RED

WHO'S AFRAID OF THE BIG BAD WOLF?

by Nicole Little

Once upon a time...

Lyall and Blanchette—small town high-school sweethearts, the envy of all their friends and perhaps, even more so, the envy of those who are *not* their friends.

As Blanchette's eighteenth birthday comes to pass, our two star-crossed lovers are married. A simple ceremony, for they are young and not yet established. They agree that there is no need for the extravagance of a fancy wedding or a lavish reception. Lyall lovingly cradles his blushing bride as he carries her over the threshold, and thus, they find themselves settling down in a small cottage bequeathed to Blanchette in her grandmother's will—a tragic story itself, the loss of dear Granny B, but a bit more about that later.

Yes, things are perfect! But as is wont to happen

when life gets just a bit *too* perfect, when people get a little too happy and content—tragedy strikes.

And things are about to get a whole lot messy.

The noise came from a distance, faint and muddled, barely discernible above the ringing in his ears. A low moan escaped his lips, a whispered word: Red.

A shout came, close by and far, far too loud. "He's over here!" A jackhammer of pain ricocheted through his head. "Lyall? Lyall, can you hear me, son?"

Suddenly he was surrounded by a chorus of worried murmurs and frantic exclamations. A mint-scented breath wafted over his face as someone leaned next to him and felt for a pulse at his neck. "Lyall, can you open your eyes for me? Help is on the way."

"Jesus, there's so much blood."

"Be quiet, Earl! He'll hear you."

But just before the darkness swamped him once again, Lyall heard the same damn voice whisper, "But if he's here alone, then where's the girl?"

Lyall's skin was slick with sweat, and his breath came in quick gasps. He ran his hands through his short dark hair—hair that had just recently begun to grey—

and glanced nervously at the shadows as they tangoed in and out of the tangled Sierra backwoods. His face flushed scarlet with exertion, he welcomed the brisk autumn breeze that rose up to greet him. The crisp leaves beneath his Blundstones crackled as he hurried along the heavily carpeted forest path. He'd convinced himself that he'd still be able to find his way to the cottage even after all these years, but now he was terribly lost. Dusk was descending, and he was decidedly alone.

Lyall rounded a particularly overgrown copse of trees and stopped short, swearing darkly under his breath—he'd been so sure this was the right direction. He placed his hands on his hips, still breathing heavily, winded by the exertion of the trek through the woods and breathless with exasperation.

His head snapped up at the splintered crack of a branch as it echoed across the clearing. Then, the thud of rapidly approaching footfalls. Lyall's heart rate accelerated, but his mind cleared as he eased himself into a defensive crouch.

"Ah, there you are, Mr Garou. We've been waiting for you."

"Mr Sanders!" Lyall relaxed as the real estate developer emerged into the clearing. "This is a little embarrassing, but I think I must have taken a wrong turn somewhere."

Sanders chuckled softly, "Easily done. It's become a bit overgrown since you've last been here, I'd imagine." He glanced around and nodded appreciatively. "But with a little work, it's going to be spectacular."

"I think so too," Lyall agreed enthusiastically.

"Well, if you will follow me, Mr Garou. It's not far from here to the cottage and we have a great many things to discuss."

Lyall rubbed his hands together. "Lead the way."

Consciousness slammed into her like the bitter slap of an ice-cold hand. There had been nothingness and then, suddenly, she was…back. Darkness was descending on the sky above her, and she could just glimpse the faint outline of a harvest moon. Though she was lying flat on her back, she recognised immediately where she was.

The woods.

Not far from the cottage.

She blinked rapidly, jumped to her feet, and brushed the brittle bits of broken leaves from her clothing. What on earth was she doing here in the middle of the forest, in the middle of the night? She felt ok, could see no injuries, she was maybe a little confused, a little chilled. She grasped the bonnet of her cape and pulled it up over her head, tucking her long crimson locks inside the hood. She tugged it close together at her neck and shivered.

A howl in the distance raised the hairs on the back of her neck, and she whipped her head in its direction. Her hand flew to her chest in alarm.

Oh.

Nothing.

That was odd.

Red tensed. Ran her fingers softly over her face.

With a start, she realised no breath crossed her lips.

Well.

That *was* rather odd indeed.

"We plan to start bulldozing as soon as possible." Sanders leaned in through his car door and retrieved a leather briefcase. "Once these papers are signed, I'll call the foreman. His crew will be here by the end of the weekend."

Lyall nodded, understanding that there was no need for a response.

Sanders gestured in the direction of the old

building. "I let myself in a little earlier while I was waiting for you. The front door was barely hanging on the hinges. The kitchen table seems sturdy enough. If you don't mind getting a bit of dust on you, we can go inside, sit down, and get everything squared away."

Go inside? An involuntary shiver raced down Lyall's spine. He hadn't been inside since…

"Sure thing," he replied, shaking off a vague sense of unease. There was nothing left in that cottage but some old cobwebs and even older memories. He trailed Sanders up the creaky steps, paused at the threshold, his eyes adjusting to the dimness inside, and then he plunged through the doorway.

One of those men looked familiar to her. Squinting, she felt a vague sense of déjà vu wash over her. Red tried to grab at the wisp of memory, but it was fleeting, just beyond her grasp. Who were these men and what were they doing at Grandmother's cottage? She drifted closer and listened at the window.

"Now sign here, and here, and put today's date right here on this line." He gestured, one finger jabbing at the paper. "Once I'm back at the office, I'll transfer the full payment to your account and voila—done deal."

The man, the one who looked so familiar to her, picked up a gold-coloured pen and signed the document with a flourish. A Cheshire grin spread across his face. He stood and offered his hand to the larger man, who was slipping the papers into a brown leather case. "Nice doing business with you, M. Sanders."

"And you too, Lyall."

Lyall.

She whispered the name to herself, tasted bitterness on her tongue.

Then it all came rushing back to her.

Anger clawed at her throat, scalded its way down into her belly where it pooled in a molten pit of rage.

She stood outside the window of the cottage, a place she had once called home. She had dared to be happy there. But that happiness had never come to fruition. She was swamped by memories of her childhood, her dear Granny B and, finally, of her brief life as a married woman.

And there *he* was. Standing in the middle of the kitchen, grinning foolishly to himself. Pleased as punch. Just like he owned the damn place.

He had *no* right.

The burning in her belly intensified. She

recognised it, embraced it. She knew what she had to do now, that much was clear. She drifted back to the cover of the misty woods and watched the man with the briefcase as he approached his fancy car, phone already at his ear.

And there she waited, biding her time, stoking the fires of revenge.

He was rich! Like, *filthy* rich. Lyall chortled gleefully to himself. He could not believe his good luck. He was finally getting his due. He scrutinised the abandoned house, the film of dust that covered every visible surface. The foetid waft of something spoiled engulfed him. A grimace of distaste crinkled his aristocratic nose, and he spat on the floor as if to somehow dislodge the taste of decay that flooded his mouth. He stepped backward and something snapped beneath his heel: a desiccated mouse carcass near the old gas range. He made a sound of disgust under his breath and decided his time here would be short. And yet, curiosity gripped him with a firm hand and he found himself wandering further inside, wanting to see just how pathetic things had grown. He poked his head through the archway leading into the lounge room. It had been small but serviceable once, but not anymore.

The large window that overlooked the orchard had been smashed out, its curtain ragged and threadbare, blowing slightly in the breeze. Years of rain and snow had warped the wooden floor and soddened the wall. A colony of black mould had taken up residence on the once pristine wallpaper, its spores spreading like a contagion. The old chintz couch sagged; stuffing spewed from underneath it, yellow globs of sponge and rusted springs. The mantel above the fireplace was draped in cobwebs. A large wedding portrait, once in a place of pride, had now shifted precariously on the wall, its frame bulging with damp and its smiling subjects corrupted with mildew and time. Lyall barely gave it a glance.

Mercifully, there was no upstairs. He rounded the corner and ahead of him, a small bathroom, and then the bedroom. The door was shut. He stood in front of it, his hand reaching out to grasp it of its own accord. He pushed against the old door, its frame creaking loudly in protest. The room was in surprisingly good condition: the bed was still made. Dust motes danced before him in the faint light of the setting sun. A silver comb and brush set sat waiting on the vanity, a demure white cotton nightgown was folded at the foot of the bed, atop a lovingly crafted handmade quilt; against the pillows rested an old stuffed toy. He backed out of the room, leaving the door open. Not that it mattered. It would all be gone in a few days. Smashed to smithereens and hauled away like yesterday's trash. Lyall could not think of a more fitting end. He smirked.

And that was when he heard the front door slam.

Rage unlike any she had ever experienced detonated inside her, and the building shuddered under the force of the door as she willed it shut. It swayed dangerously back and forth on its rusted hinges, threatening to fall. But Red, blue flames flickering at her fingertips, clenched her hand into a fist and the entrance sealed itself tight. A surge of energy coursed through her. She raised her hands and lowered the bonnet of her cape, shook out her long curly hair. It gleamed, lustrous in the dusky light, illuminated by the gleam of the moon and the light that emanated from inside her.

Red saw the flash of shock in Lyall's eyes as he charged into the room and as he took full stock of her standing before him. He recovered quickly; his surprise replaced by smug satisfaction. He straightened his shoulders, slid his hands into his pockets, and rocked back and forth on his heels—the picture of nonchalance. "How d'you pull it off?"

"Irrelevant." Red's voice was gravelly from disuse, as though the earth beneath which she had been buried was still stuck in her throat. It was a fact that she had no idea what had returned her to this place, but she had no intentions of letting Lyall know that.

He snorted in derision, "A deal with the devil, I suppose."

"No. But that would be no worse than the deal I signed when I married you."

Lyall's eyes narrowed, but he did not acknowledge the remark. "So, what…you think coming back here now is going to change anything? I'm not afraid of ghosts."

Red's hands sparked, and her eyes flashed a brilliant azure. "Perhaps you should be."

Lyall's nostrils flared and Red suspected she was about to see the *real* man she'd married – who, it had turned out, wasn't really a man at all.

"You think you're special, *Blanchette*? Because you are not. I had many before you and I will have more again once I send you back where you came from. Back with your stupid bitch grandmother."

"What?" Red recoiled, shock and confusion. Static electricity snapped in the air and Red's hair crackled in response. Lyall smirked. He knew he'd hit home. Behind his full lying lips, Red could see that his canines had already begun to lengthen. Noticing the direction of her gaze, he ran his tongue over them suggestively.

Red was barely able to suppress a shudder.

"I suppose there's no harm in telling you now. Not like you can do anything about it. Yes. *Your* grandmother. Poor Granny B. And damn, was she ever delicious." He threw back his head and laughed. "And you had absolutely no idea. You even *married* me! Who's the sicko now?"

"But…but that's just not possible."

"Sorry, doll, but you knew you were marrying an *older* man…it just happened to be a lot older than you thought." He had the nerve to look pleased with himself. "A *lot* older. You see, I need to feed occasionally to maintain my youthful exuberance. Not often, mind you, but after I'd sampled your grandmother…" He moaned in delight, Red could see saliva glistening at the corners of his mouth. "And then I saw luscious little Blanchette bawling her eyes out at the funeral. Well, I knew all I had to do was bide my time. A few years and then I could have you too. When you were old enough. So, I enrolled at the school and you couldn't resist. The fucking was a nice bonus."

In a flash of certainty, Red realised exactly what Lyall was trying to do—trying to rattle her, so she'd make a stupid mistake or let down her guard. It might have worked on a once innocent Blanchette, but the Red that stood here now, well, that was entirely different. An eerie calm settled over her and she smiled serenely at him. "You give yourself too much credit, *husband*, it wasn't that much of a bonus for me."

Oh boy, *that* did it. She'd beaten him at his own game.

A snarl of rage erupted from deep within his chest. His nails elongated and tufts of bristling fur began to emerge on his chest and hands. Red could tell he was struggling to keep control of the change. And ordinarily, control was something Lyall was very good at.

He launched himself at her, all teeth and claws for just a brief moment, allowing his baser instincts to take over, and forgetting that, despite what he saw right in front of him, Red was merely an apparition. She closed her eyes and simply willed herself across the room, and the beast that was Lyall slammed headfirst into the wall. Snarling, spittle flying from his mouth, he cursed at her in a guttural language that sounded older than time.

His eyes narrowed to slits as he faced her, breathing ragged, nostrils flared.

"Oh, Lyall. I'm learning just what my strengths are in this new ethereal body of mine. It's quite fascinating, actually. Like this, for example."

She vanished. He frantically searched the room; his vision had sharpened considerably since the change had begun, but the dark recesses at the far reaches of the tiny home still remained cloaked in smoky shadows.

The rake of razor-sharp nails down the side of his face—the slicing of skin across one eye—quickly brought him back to reality, and he roared in pain and frustration. Red blinked back into existence, across the room again, a satisfied grin eclipsing her face. "Isn't that a neat trick?"

He growled. His tone low and hoarse, more beast than man now. "You'll pay for that, bitch."

"I'll *pay*?" She laughed, a light tinkling sound. "Haven't I already *paid*, dear husband? You think that I do not recall with stunning clarity the feel of your teeth against my throat, the rip and tear of my own flesh; choking on the warm blood as you gorged yourself? I watched you, you know, as you dragged what was left of my mutilated body, back to your lair. A midnight snack perhaps."

"Was it you then?" he exclaimed, snuffling rapidly through his elongating snout. "You who knocked me out and left me in the clearing that night?"

"Goodness me, Lyall. Did you almost get caught? Tsk, tsk, tsk. Were you a bit off your game?"

"Hardly," he scoffed, then sneered. "I'd been resting. That's always nice after a big meal."

In a flash, she was behind him. Her bare foot slammed into the small of his back and Lyall sprawled across the rotting floor in a crumpled heap. He jumped to all fours and then scrambled to two feet, roaring, already lashing out. What was left of the windows in the old cottage rattled in their frames, but he snatched at empty air. Red was nowhere to be seen.

"I'm in here," she called in a singsong voice.

The bedroom.

Lyall scrambled down the hall, clicking as he ran, his pointed toenails having burst through the front of his boots. The door was closed—like he'd found it earlier. From behind the entrance, he could hear the faint sounds of Red humming an upbeat tune. He cocked his head. It sounded an awful lot like "Don't Stop Me Now" by Queen. He'd always hated that song.

He tried the latch. Locked. He dragged his talons down the wooden door, leaving deep gouges. "You going to make me knock this down?" he snapped.

The humming stopped. With a scream of protest, the door opened inwards excruciatingly slowly, revealing Red illuminated in the glow of a kerosene lamp. She was sitting at the edge of the bed, cradling a rag doll in her hands. "You know, Granny B gave me this doll for my first Christmas." She glanced at him from beneath her lashes. "She had the exact same coloured hair as me, so I called her Little Red. I dragged her everywhere with me. I've missed her."

"Is there a point to this story?" Lyall drawled.

"No." Red smiled. "Just a distraction really."

"A distraction?" he trailed off, his senses on high alert. Still in the doorway, he hesitated to step across the threshold. Despite his proclivity for violence, his strength and stamina, Lyall felt a frisson of fear inch its way down his spine. Then, from the corner of his eye: a shimmer, the vague outline of a shape that hadn't been there before. His gaze shot back to Red, but she was still where she had been a moment ago, sitting on the end of the bed, a smile on her face as she stroked the hair of that stupid doll.

Bam. Something slammed into him from behind

with the force of a battering ram and he flew into the room, tumbling head over tail across the floor until he rammed up against the antique vanity; the mirror above him shattered, raining sharp fragments of reflective glass down on top of him, where they glittered in his burgeoning fur.

"Oh, no," Red intoned, dripping with scorn. "That's seven years' bad luck for you now, Lyall."

"Who…what…how did you do that?" he demanded. For one so used to always being in control, his quavering tone betrayed just how out of his element he was—sitting on the floor, blood dripping into his eye, torn pants, darting furtive glances over his shoulder.

"Not me, darling."

"Hello, Lyall, dear." The voice was like sandpaper, rough from years of disuse but clear and unmistakable. He would have recognised it anywhere. "Aren't you going to welcome me back?"

That shimmer again. Then it slowly began to take shape. Soft edges became sharper and suddenly there she was, standing next to Red, a supportive hand on her granddaughter's shoulder.

Granny B.

"Isn't this nice?" she asked in her soft lilting

accent. "The whole family back together again."

Granny B and Red exchanged a knowing glance, and all at once, Lyall knew with absolute certainty he'd never get to spend a cent of his recent windfall. Before he could even scramble to his feet—the weak, pathetic attempt to escape that it was—they were upon him, slashing and scratching, gouging and tearing; their high-pitched squeals of laughter and ecstatic cackles were deafening, and Lyall felt a sharp pain on both sides of his head as his eardrums burst. Blood flowed freely from his nose and into his mouth—he made no attempt to wipe it away. Lyall felt himself revert back to human form as he weakened. Defenceless now, he lay cowering in a ball on the floor, sobbing as the skin was flayed from his back. He felt the bone in his ankle snap as one of the two wrenched it with a twist. He screamed.

When the frenzy had ended, when Lyall was simply a pile of ragged flesh and jagged bones beneath them, Red and Granny B looked at each other with delighted smiles.

"Granny B, you have something in your hair."

She made an ineffective swipe at her ghostly grey hair.

"Let me get that for you," Red said indulgently as

she picked a small object from her grandmother's wavy locks. "Oh. It's just a tooth!" Both of them dissolved into peals of laughter, their forms dimming and brightening with the surge of emotions. Finally, recovered from their mirth, Red asked soberly, "So, what's next?"

"Well, my darling, for now we are done. Come Monday morning though, we will have much more work on our hands, won't we? We can't let those naughty men with their big machines destroy our home."

"I like the way you think, Granny! We will stay here then?" she asked, hopefully.

Red sensed a sudden charge in the air. She noticed a faint darkening of the divine aura that surrounded her grandmother, and a twinge of unease, perhaps even of fear, slid down her back.

"We will indeed, my sweet. We are tied to this place, together forever, you and I." Granny B grinned.

"My goodness, Grandmother," she said as she turned to face the woman who sat across from her at the kitchen table. "What big teeth you have!"

Granny flashed her granddaughter a very wide, very satisfied smile. "All the better to…well, I think you know how the story goes, right, Red?"

GILLIAN

ETERNAL VENGEANCE

by Maxine Churchman

Cold and alone. Wrenched from my mother's arms, so soon after being reunited, and back in the world I left behind. A sadness aches deep within me.

I remember so little of my passing: the warmth of the water, the sting of the blade across my wrist—resignation.

The face of my husband springs to mind. Doctor Kevin Roper. I was so proud to be a doctor's wife. I was looking forward to a life of glittering parties and theatre shows, but he chose a General Practice in Yorkshire.

In a blink, I am in the house I hated so much, on the edge of the Yorkshire Dales. The wind moans under the doors and rattles the kitchen window. I look out and see the familiar trees—bare now—they point skyward like accusing skeletons from the afterlife. "Go back," they seem to say, and I wish I could. The undulating fields, stretching for miles, are dotted with sheep and crisscrossed by crumbling dry-stone walls that follow the steep contours. I watch as dark clouds boil over the peaks and roll down the slopes, enveloping everything in a grey mist. I remember this view, remote and bleak. Despite the heavy clouds, the grass begins to look green instead of grey and I realise it must be dawn.

A key turns in the lock and my heart surges, just as it used to when Kevin was home. I rush to the hallway. He is so handsome with his dark curly hair and neat beard. His grey eyes look tired. Has a call out to a wealthy client kept him from his bed again? And him in mourning, he is so dedicated. He removes his coat with a shrug of his shoulders, and I absentmindedly take it from him, but my hands pass straight through. I turn to the hall mirror and see a pale image of myself reflected back. The crack in the wall behind me is visible through my body making it look as though I am broken in half. Kevin hurries upstairs, taking them two at a time. He didn't see me. I touch my mousy hair, cut in a short bob, and smooth the front of my thin slip over my flat stomach. I feel the same, but as I hold out my hands, I can see through them.

As Kevin showers, I try picking up items from the

hall table, but no matter how much I concentrate, my hand just passes straight through. In frustration, I swipe my arm across the top of the table. A tall vase wobbles ever so slightly.

Kevin rushes down the stairs, depositing a black tie over the end of the banister. He is smartly dressed in a dark suit and stops to check his appearance in the hall mirror. He flicks a curl into place. He turns and strides to the kitchen, passing straight through me. The shock as we align affects us both, leaving me disorientated as I try to process what happened. He shivered. I felt his heartbeat and the warmth of his blood. I also saw an image of Mary Braithwaite, her lips full and red with desire.

Jealousy and rage taste like sour milk, I run my tongue around my mouth, unable to move while I work through the thoughts in my head. I hear him blundering around the kitchen, filling the kettle, opening and shutting cupboards. Has he forsaken my love so soon after my death? My world seems to shrink around me.

A sharp rap on the front door makes me jump. Kevin passes through me again on his way to open it, and I taste annoyance.

He pulls open the door, his shoulders sag slightly. "Hello, Ron. You're a little early, I've just put the kettle on," he says, standing to one side.

Daddy—big, brash, and dashing—enters, and I give in to my misery. If only he would pull me into his embrace and tell me everything is OK. He never did when I was alive, so why should he now? He doesn't even see me.

He pats Kevin's shoulder. "You shouldn't be alone today, son. And you shouldn't blame yourself. She never really got over the trauma of her mother's death. She always thought it was her fault."

Anger churns in my stomach like a beast about to strike. *He* blamed me for her death—he couldn't bear to look at me. I expel my fury, screaming in his face like a dragon breathing fire. I am disappointed by his indifference, although I think I perceive a slight paling of his complexion.

Daddy walks through me, and I detect a deep sadness. Perhaps I misunderstood him. He pauses and turns. "Your house is cold. Perhaps you should turn up the heating."

Kevin stops just in front of me, his brow creased. Can he feel my presence? I reach up to smooth the lines, but he surges forward, too quickly for me to savour his warmth.

I watch them drinking coffee in the kitchen. Stilted

conversation punctuates long periods of awkward silence until more people arrive. I don't know them; they are probably friends or colleagues of Kevin's. They all shake his hand or embrace him, murmuring how sorry they are for his loss. A pretty blonde girl holds him longer than seems appropriate and blushes as they pull apart. As she walks into me, I go with her, keeping pace. She gasps and pulls her shawl closer. I feel her heart quicken—she's thinking about how desirable my husband is and wondering how long he'll be in mourning.

I return to the hallway where Kevin is admitting Mary Braithwaite. I hate how attractive she is with her wavy red hair and sparkling green eyes. She presses herself against him as she passes through the front door. They don't speak or hug. He simply stands still while she retrieves his tie from the banister and ties it around his neck. There is something very intimate about the moment, as if this is a ritual they have performed many times, and I wonder how long they have been seeing each other.

She wraps her arms around his neck, and he takes her wrists, removing them. She looks hurt.

"I'll introduce you to my father-in-law," he says. "You know what to do."

She makes a face, like a child being told to tidy her room. I walk into her and she catches her breath.

"Are you OK?" Kevin asks.

I feel her knees buckle and let her go. I gleaned enough to know they spent last night, and many others, together. She recovers and they head into the other room.

The hearse and cars arrive, and everyone spills out of the house.

At the crematorium, I stand behind the vicar as he drones. None of my London friends are here. I haven't seen them since my wedding.

Kevin tells everyone what a wonderful wife I was, and how much he misses me. I move towards him. It would be fun to make him shudder in front of his crowd, but he stuns me by saying his only regret is that he wasn't there to prevent me from taking my own life.

He *was* there. I remember. I remember it all now; he pressed the blade against my wrist. I was too tired to fight—drugged for certain.

The room spins, so many unknown faces swirl around me. Trembling, I leave the chapel.

There is a woman standing beside the trunk of an ancient oak tree some twenty metres away. She is wearing a long figure-hugging dress of dark green with long bell-shaped sleeves. Her eyes, also green, shine eerily from the shade of a large hood.

She takes one step and appears directly in front of me, like a film with several frames missing. I am startled and move away, but she grabs my wrist with slender fingers—they feel cool and strong. I can't see her face, but her eyes are mesmerising.

"You do not belong here," she says in a deep voice that causes unpleasant vibrations to travel from her fingers to my chest. "Your soul is clean. Why are you here?" she demands.

"I don't know. I would gladly go back if I could." I yearn to be with my mother again. There is nothing for me here.

She drops my wrist. "I am Demosa. I could help you. What is your given name?"

Relief buoys me. "Gillian. Please—help me."

She places a finger between my eyes. Images, symbols and words flash through my mind too fast to fathom. "Avenge your death. Recite the incantation I have given you as spirit and body separate. When you are avenged, a second incantation will take you to where you should be."

Her words trouble me. How can I kill my husband?

"Find a way," she says, reading my thoughts.

Her eyes blaze and she is gone, leaving me feeling scared and shaky.

Back at our house, caterers have laid out sandwiches and cakes on the dining table, and people are helping themselves to food and drink while they chat and laugh. I find Daddy in the living room, lounging on the sofa, chatting to Mary. They seem to be getting on very well; she is laughing at his jokes and frequently touching his upper arm while thrusting her chest provocatively towards him. His eyes keep flicking down to her cleavage but she, I notice, keeps seeking out Kevin. A knowing look passes between them, they are up to something.

The guests start leaving in small groups until only Mary, Kevin, and Daddy are left. Mary offers to stay and clear up, but Kevin hauls her off the sofa and almost pushes her into the hall.

"Thanks. It's all taken care of," he says in a tone that allows no rebuttal. The look she gives him could curdle milk and their disharmony gives me some comfort.

Daddy stays on the sofa, a dazed look in his eyes. "I'll call you tomorrow, honey," he calls, enunciating each syllable.

Mary presses her lips together and glares at Kevin. He kisses her gently on the cheek and whispers in her ear, "You did well. I love you."

She kisses him on the lips and leaves.

Kevin whisks around the rooms, clearing up the leftover food and dirty plates. I itch to help him, or at least instruct him how to do it properly. It is too frustrating watching him though, and I swap my attention to Daddy. He has fallen asleep and is snoring softly. I have a desire to be close to him, so I sit down aligning myself to his body. At first, he snorts and moves, his brow creases. A shudder runs through his body, but I sit still, and he relaxes again. I move slowly to position my head where his is, then I concentrate on our fingers, and finally our feet. Daddy is much larger than me, but I find I can expand and lengthen myself to fit. I close my eyes and think about how I am wearing Daddy like a second skin. Images flash in my mind and I realise I am seeing his dream. He is dreaming of Mum, how beautiful and popular she was. Her radiant smile, the love in her eyes, it is all there in his dream. She smiles at him as they do the dishes together; that must have been very early days, before the business boomed and he spent all his time at the office. They are walking in a park, hand in hand, and he is so happy. They sit down on a bench and he turns to look at her. She has changed into Mary Braithwaite. I recoil and the image disintegrates. I start to get up, but his body comes with me. Shocked, I sit back. I lift one arm, turning the hand over, and his arm moves at my command. It feels heavy. I run the fingers along the arm of the sofa, but I don't feel the texture of the cloth. It is like wearing a heavy rubber glove. I open my mouth and his mouth opens. I tire of the game and panic as I realise I can't disengage from him.

Kevin enters the room with a couple of mugs of tea. "Ron! Are you OK?" He puts the drinks down and waves his hand in front of Daddy's eyes. He peers into them and I worry he will see me. I shrink back from his critical stare. The move frees me.

Daddy shudders and sits forward with his head in his hands. "That was a really weird dream."

Kevin pats his shoulder. "I was about to get the medical bag. Have you had seizures before?"

"Seizures?" He looks up, alarmed. "No, no. I was only asleep."

"OK, but get your doctor to give you the once over, just to be sure."

Daddy looks very pale, whether from my

possession or the idea he might be having seizures, I don't know. He just nods.

"You were getting on well with Mary," Kevin says in a bright voice that sounds a little brittle to my ears.

Daddy grins and blushes. I've never seen him do that before. "She's a lovely girl. Do you think I am mad? She's half my age."

"No, of course not. You are a good-looking chap and fitter than a lot of men half your age."

"I haven't even thought of dating since Evelyn passed." His hands shake and he clasps them together.

"You don't want to be lonely going forward. Once you retire, having a younger companion will keep you young."

Daddy laughs. "She can help me spend the money when I sell the company."

Things start to make sense, and I don't like where my thoughts are taking me.

The two men chat and laugh like a couple of college friends. If I wasn't dead, and if I didn't suspect what Kevin was planning, it would warm my heart, but as I listen to their conversation, I see what a master of manipulation my husband is, and it makes me re-evaluate the time we spent together, before and during our marriage.

A little while after Daddy leaves, there is a gentle tap on the window. Kevin races to open the door. He pushes it shut behind Mary and they kiss passionately, thrusting their bodies together and writhing. She runs her hands through his hair, and he digs his fingers into her ample buttocks, making her gasp and groan.

He has never kissed me like that, and I feel empty and betrayed.

They release each other and Mary races up the stairs squealing as Kevin laughs and smacks her rear. I stand at the bottom of the stairs, trying not to listen to the sex noises they make.

How would Daddy feel if he knew about Mary and Kevin?

As soon as it goes quiet upstairs, I enter the bedroom. They are cuddling in bed: her head on his chest, his hand stroking her hair tenderly. They could be any one of a million couples, but they are my husband and his lover. It is obvious they have been intimate for a long time. I am humiliated, thinking about all the times I waited up for him while he was probably with her. I am considering my next move when she speaks.

"Darling, I don't want to marry Ron," she says in

a small voice.

I see the dreamy look leave Kevin's face and his hand stops moving. "Come on, love, be strong. I married Gillian."

I freeze.

"So you know how hard it will be for me," she whines. "If you hadn't killed her so soon, I wouldn't need to prostitute myself to Ron."

The room spins. Her words hit me like a blow to the stomach. They had planned everything together.

He grabs a handful of her hair, pulling her back onto the pillow, and looms over her. The muscles in his jaw ripple. "I had no choice," he says through gritted teeth. "You know she was insisting we move back to London, everything would have been spoilt."

He rolls off the bed and heads for the en suite, leaving Mary looking small and frightened.

When the shower starts, Mary relaxes a little. She is staring at the ceiling, her eyes flicking as though she is deep in thought. I ease myself onto the bed, quickly aligning myself with her form before she can move. She lets out a small gasp, but I have her. I keep still and relax, waiting for her thoughts to appear to me like Daddy's dreams did. I visualise Kevin on our wedding day, prompting her memories to come tumbling forth in a torrent of mixed emotions. One image repeats often with great tenderness and a feeling of loss: Kevin saying goodbye at the station as he heads to medical college. It seems everything changed in her mind at that point in time. Before, their love was pure and simple. After, she became the other woman, but still his only love. I can taste her contempt for me. She was torn, wanting Kevin to inherit my father's wealth but not wanting him to give himself to me. I experience her hope and elation at my death, and I lose control of my own emotions. There is so much hatred and wrath boiling inside me, the pressure builds, like steam in a sealed container, I thrash and scream letting it out lest I explode. Mary's body bucks and twists, tangling in the covers, knocking over the bedside lamp, rapping knuckles on the carved wooden headboard. At last, I am spent—as insignificant as smoke. I draw myself in and leave her panting and sobbing, her eyes darting wildly around the room. She scrambles from the bed and pulls on jeans and a jumper, then hurriedly gathers up her underwear as Kevin enters, towelling his hair. She spins round at the sound of the door opening and sobs when she sees him.

He throws the towel on a chair and rushes round the bed to her. "What's up?"

She backs away. "She's here." Her voice is barely audible. She reaches for the door, but he grabs her upper arm. She shakes him off. "Gillian is here. I felt her. She wants to kill us." She runs down the stairs.

He follows. "Ghosts! Really, Mary. There are no such things as ghosts."

"Don't," I hear her say before the front door slams.

The next day I follow Kevin to his house calls. He arrives at Mrs Skinner's cottage and is admitted by a middle-aged woman with mousy hair and badly applied makeup. Her skin is pale and lined.

"How is the old girl today, Susan?" Kevin asks.

"She had a bad night, Dr Roper, so she is in a bit of a mood."

"Kevin—please," he says with a self-deprecating smile.

Despite her age, she blushes like a schoolgirl and wrings her hands as she shuffles to the bottom of the stairs. "Mother!" she yells. "Dr Roper is here."

An indistinguishable groan comes from upstairs.

Susan stands to one side. "You know where to go—Kevin." She laughs nervously, her eyes dropping demurely to the floor. "I'll put the kettle on for when you're finished."

Upstairs, Mrs Skinner is reclining in bed, propped up with lots of frilly white pillows. She looks in rude health to me, with glowing skin and soft grey hair arranged in neat curls.

Kevin sits on a wooden chair next to the bed and takes her hand. His fawning sickens me, and I wander round the room to the window overlooking the garden. Susan is outside, pegging out some sheets. Her movements are quick and efficient, like she has no time to lose.

"—a lazy girl." Mrs Skinner's words interrupt my thoughts. "She has hidden my bell, you know? Said I was abusing her good will. How ungrateful is that? She just doesn't appreciate how ill I am."

Kevin has his stethoscope in his ears, taking her blood pressure, though how he can hear her pulse over her whining I don't know. He writes something in his notebook and puts everything in his bag.

"With me as your doctor, you will outlive us all," he reassures her and stands to leave.

"Goodness! Are you finished already? You will have to stay for some tea next time. I will get Susan to bring it up. It will give her something to do."

He leaves with a smile. I stay.

I take possession of Mrs Skinner. Her heart flutters

erratically; perhaps she will have a heart attack. I wander through her thoughts for a while, but there is nothing of interest. I open her mouth and scream as loudly as her puny lungs allow—the sound is like a tomcat's song. I hear heavy footsteps hurrying up the stairs and Kevin bursts in with his bag already partially open.

His eyes are wide and frantic. "What's wrong?" He reaches for my wrist.

Susan enters behind him, stooped and still wringing her hands.

I lunge for Kevin, placing pudgy fingers round his throat and squeeze. I laugh, but it sounds more like panting. Susan pulls on my arms while Kevin tries to pry my fingers off. I don't want to kill him—not yet—so I let go and allow Mrs Skinner to flop back on the pillows as I disengage.

As I accompany Kevin on the rest of his rounds, I become aware of just how devious he is. I practise possession with his clients after he leaves. Their reactions vary and some put up quite a fight, but I learn ways to subdue their spirit. I am horrified by how many of his clients have written him into their wills.

At the end of his round, he calls on Mary. She still

looks pale from last night. I am careful to avoid touching her as I don't want her to know I am here.

I sit with them as they eat dinner and make plans for their future. Daddy has invited Mary to London for the weekend.

"Just enjoy yourself. He will take you to great restaurants and plays."

"Mmm, that will be fun. You never take me anywhere interesting."

He looks at her through narrowed eyes. "Don't sleep with him. Tell him you are saving yourself for the wedding night."

She shudders. "Ha. You think he'll believe that?"

He grabs her wrist—his knuckles are white. "Make him."

I act quickly, possessing him decisively, not allowing him a chance to fight back. I tighten his grip on her wrist, hearing but not feeling the bones break.

She screams and sobs, trying to release her wrist, but I hang on. I don't cower when she looks into my eyes. Hers widen in terror and she grabs a fork from the table, jabbing it in my neck. I don't feel it, but Kevin's spirit bucks and a feral cry of pain escapes his mouth. I bite his tongue hard and clamp down on his rebellion. An image in his mind nearly undoes me: my naked body, lifeless in a bath of blood-red water. He reeks of contempt.

I pick up a knife in a hand slick with blood from his neck wound, and ram it into Mary's abdomen, aiming upwards. I twist and pull it out again. Kevin lurches, threatening to dislodge me but he is weakened by the blood loss—perhaps the fork caught an artery.

I let go of Mary's wrist. She slumps to the floor, a trickle of blood escaping from the corner of her mouth. Kevin is heavy, but I manage to throw him out of the chair, and he lands on top of Mary, forcing the breath from her lungs in a small, anguished sob.

I swap the knife to his right hand and slowly slide the blade over his wrist, pressing down as hard as I can, right down to the bone. I sense the pain and loathing in his spirit as I watch the dark blood spread along the floor and coat Mary's hair. I let his head drop, with a bang, next to hers and leave his body.

After a few moments, his spirit emerges and turns hateful eyes on me. I recite the incantation imprinted in my brain—harsh guttural sounds that mean nothing to me. His spirit is enveloped by a sickly green light that pulses and shrinks; he pushes against it but is cowed into a crouch. On the last syllable, his spirit and the light disappear.

Mary hangs in there. Her breathing is shallow and ragged under the weight of Kevin. I wonder if his body is pressing on her wound, stopping her from bleeding out. I am not inclined to possess his corpse, so I watch and wait.

When her spirit finally emerges, it gives in to the green light without a struggle.

Vengeance has not brought the elation I expected. A knot of pain resides where my heart used to be. I want to feel Mum's arms around me again. I am ready to return. I recite the second incantation. The words are softer, but just as strange. As I utter the last few syllables, Demosa appears. She pulls back her hood to reveal a hideously misshapen head with three short horns and what looks like writhing rats' tails for hair. I try to step back and find I cannot move.

"Welcome to my parlour," she says, sweeping her arms wide.

All around us are rows of long shelves, like a huge library, but instead of books, there are countless various sized ginger jars. Most of them are emitting a green mist that is sucked into a large bell jar in the centre of the room, where it condenses into thick goo.

"I'd like to go back now, please," I say. "I have done as you instructed."

"You have." She smiles, revealing rows of tiny needle-like teeth. "That is why you belong here—your soul is no longer pure—and with the incantations, you gifted me your murderers and yourself. I will feast on your vengeance for eternity." She licks her lips and removes the lid of a jar. I feel it pulling me and I try to resist. My hands and arms lengthen and thin as they, followed by the rest of my body, are drawn into the jar, like smoke up a chimney.

I am in a bedroom holding a large knife in both hands above my head. Mary and Kevin lie on the bed in each other's arms. There is fear in their eyes, but they make no effort to move. Perhaps, like me, they can't. Against my will, I plunge the knife into them, and as I do, I feel the excruciating pain of the metal slicing through flesh and bone as if it is my own. My cry of pain mixes with their screams. I lift the knife high and plunge it into them again, and again. Each time the agony intensifies, and our screams amplify until the room is filled with one long sound of anguish and pain. At last, they are silent, and I collapse in an exhausted heap on their mutilated bodies. We are enveloped by a green mist that rises and disappears.

Again, I am in the bedroom holding the knife

above my head. Mary and Kevin cling to each other, looking terrified. I plunge the knife into them over and over, crying out against the searing pain, adding my voice to their awful screams until they are silent, and I collapse on their bodies. The green mist is all around.

I am back on my feet with the knife over my head. Mary and Kevin look horrified. I know what is coming, but I am unable to change a thing. I tense, in anticipation of the terrible pain, I cry out in unison with them. At last, they are silent, and I fall on them, aware once more of the green mist.

I stand. Mary and Kevin cower. The knife cuts. We scream. I collapse. Mist ascends.

Is this my existence now? Agony and clamour without end, in a perpetual green fog. Cut and scream, cut and scream…

AVA

IMMORTAL DESPISED

by Beth W. Patterson

The branch swayed more violently than usual in the autumnal wind, but Ava did not lose her grip. And if she did, it wasn't as if she would tumble to the ground. But she had already fallen, whether from grace or dignity, she did not know.

Is this what I have been reduced to? she wondered. *Can a single human demote the music of my divine lineage to a simple folk song?*

But the stout figure with the wild, unkempt hair was no ordinary person. Ava had observed him strolling these woods near Vienna for weeks. She did not mind his pockmarked face or dishevelled attire. So unlike any man she had ever seen wandering this territory, he could almost be one of her ilk! His careful attention to every detail in the wilderness made her feel a connection to another living creature for the first time. And she had always been so alone in the world.

Ava launched herself into the air, soared above his head, and poured her heart out with trills and warbles. Her species was not a flashy-looking bird, and she was equally plain in human form. But celebrated by Ovid, Chaucer, Shakespeare, nightingales had become symbols of poets and poetry through their naturally melodious calls. They did not need to rely on their looks for adoration by mankind. True nightingales didn't even concern themselves with such things.

A yearning for human connection burned in her tiny breast. But she quelled it with the rationale that she had tried to carefully cultivate over the years. She had tried to spend as much time in bird form as possible, for human emotions were dangerous and in her heritage lurked a vengeful streak. She was a direct descendant of Philomela, a mortal woman of ancient Greece who had become pregnant just before the gods transformed her into a nightingale. The first egg laid by the bird hatched the forerunner of all nightingale shapeshifters.

She was grateful that this was a natural part of her very biology. She did not need to use a transformation spell like that famous Scottish witch Isobel Gowdie, who had given herself to the devil. But Ava's blood was still both a blessing and a curse.

The nightingale shifter's predecessor, nearly reduced to a myth, had had her tongue ripped out while she was still a woman, and after that, only the males of the true species sang. Philomela's female scions, however, had much to say. A monomorphic species, nightingale males and females looked the same, and thus the shifters were able to sing their hearts out without anyone noticing the aberrant behaviour.

Could Ava rise above the anger encoded in her genetics, breaking a toxic chain that had spanned millennia?

A second figure trailing her mortal fixation wandered into view. She had never seen him in this area before. His gait was careful and purposeful, his head swinging from side to side like a lost fox pup frantically looking for its mother. He too scribbled onto a sheet of music paper, but he had turned his ice-blue eyes fully on her. Perhaps he did not know that he was plagiarising a bird's song meant for only one pair of ears.

The walking stick he carried seemed out of place. It was too heavy to be of real use, and this was an able-bodied man. The silver handle forged in the shape of a lion's head, jewelled red eyes glittering in the sunlight. Did this man merely fancy ornate objects, or was he involved in more sinister matters?

She took a chance and leapt from her spot, fluttering down to materialise as a woman, placing herself between the interloper and the mysterious object of her fascination. Her hair always fell loosely with the transition, feathers morphing into a simple gauzy gown of grey silk, atypical of the fashion these modern Austrian women favoured these days in the early 1800s.

If this strange man was surprised by her transformation, he hid it well. All other humans she saw were too concerned with social mores, fashion, and hierarchy. This newcomer saw not a barefooted woman, but something special.

"Your songs are what we need in this world," he whispered. "Nature's design is far more timeless and lovely than that…considerable novelty," he continued, indicating the slovenly eccentric retreating into the woods out of sight.

How dare this newcomer criticise the man who had so fascinated her? "And I suppose you are some sort of musical expert?"

His eyes softened, as if seeing her all over again.

"My name is Benedikt Schindler, and I have struggled to be a composer for longer than you can imagine. That man you see gets all the glory and attention, but I can assure you that he is quite mad. If you don't believe me, just follow him to his home and watch him through his window."

She flew back up to the branch, unwilling to shatter the perfection of the myth she had already created in her mind.

Schindler hummed a melody and tipped his hat. "When you are ready to make your gifts known to the world, even outshining the likes of him," he purred, "I will happily facilitate your rise to greatness. Observe him and learn. You will eventually receive a sign that will indicate exactly where to find me, should you choose to do so."

And with that, he moved along without a backward glance.

Leaving the woods was a daunting experience for her. There were fewer hiding places in the city, and too many people wandered the cobblestoned streets. She had seen horses before but was slightly frightened by how the animals were harnessed to giant wheeled boxes, how men urged them to do their bidding.

Winter was approaching fast, and normally, she would have migrated to Africa by now. But she had been unable to resist following the strange man to his home in Vienna. She spied him through the window of a tiny upstairs apartment in a gargantuan blockish house.

Immersed in his piano keys, his world had become precise and binary, a black and white landscape from which volcanic spectrums erupted forth. And the silences in between the notes were the atoms that held the universe together.

Ava had never heard such music. She had had no childhood. She recalled little of her life as a fledgling, and then one day, she had simply stepped into the sunlight as a young woman. When one spends half of life in animal form, human emotions can become blurred. Whatever it was that stirred her was more than mating songs of birds, insects, and frogs. It was the sound of creation itself.

She would have to spend more time as a lady if she were to fully grasp the polyphony. It was a risk, for she would have to sacrifice the safety that was the innocence of her nightingale mind. Was she equipped to take on the burdens she had watched mortals struggle with: their jealousies and grudges, their neuroses and regrets?

She had yet to learn that lost causes are the songs

that claim emotional territory, one's own place in the world. And the act of spilling another's blood can be an ode to joy.

🕊

6th January, Vienna, morning

My tormentor, my devil, my muse,

Am I so physically different from you that we could not be compatible? I would learn to adjust.

Temptation always lies within reach to destroy that which I cannot be a part of. But that would be the easy way. I will better myself, forge my way in a world that has no place for me, and I would do anything to have you by my side as I go forth...

🕊

Time passed, and still she observed the man she heard his servants call "Herr Beethoven."

She was puzzled as to why his employees seemed to become agitated. It was obvious that he had a digestive problem, but her animal mind did not find bodily functions to be revolting. Even when his behaviour became increasingly fascinating and frightening, with outbursts over being interrupted, she knew it was because he was trying to survive somehow.

Other things she could not understand, such as his habit of pouring water over his head. And he often howled, sometimes what seemed to be the name of a woman. Other times it was simply "My immortal beloved!"

Such a bizarre method he used to transcribe! The legs of his piano had been completely sawn off, and he lay with his ear to the floor, banging one note and then the next.

Is he...deaf? She recognised the way he picked up vibrations, much in the way that snakes did.

I can no longer remain safe and curious, she thought. *The time has come to emerge from my shell, to understand the human world in all of its complexity. I will risk this genetic proclivity.*

Suddenly she had many questions. Whom could she turn to? Then she recalled the man in the woods, who had passed no judgement on her shapeshifting nature. *Benedikt Schindler*...yes, that was his name. He'd said that she would know how to find him. What did that even mean? She hadn't even given him any thought whatsoever. All she had done since her first encounter was stare into the composer's window, reduced to an obsessive little creature.

Her tiny breast went tight with frustration before she realised she was not the only person to eavesdrop. A man who seemed to display swank plumage...no, that wasn't the right word…*clothing*…also appeared to listen. His stance was noble, but his eyes were sad, like an elderly peacock's.

"This man is a puzzle that society either wants to solve or discard," the man muttered to himself. "What has become of me? The government deems me a prince, yet I am no more than a *fenstergucker,* just like the carving on the pulpit of *Stephansdom.* I could listen to this music until I turn to stone, anonymous and forever observant."

Was this the sign that Schindler had foretold? She let forth a tiny chirp in amusement. Of course. She was a *fenstergucker,* a window gawker, just like this man. She did not know the location of *Stephansdom,* or St Stephen's Cathedral, but luckily for her, she could literally attain a bird's-eye view of the city. Perhaps that's where Schindler would be.

…Immortal muse, your cruelty knows no bounds. I would hand you the keys to the kingdom if I could, and still it is obvious that you are forever besotted by another. My social standing cannot hold a candle to the one who has captured your heart…

From her vantage point high in the air, she could

see the streets becoming a tighter grid, blocks that seemed to turn inward to face a central focal point. It was likely that something as important as Stephansdom would be in this centre. The church's impressive tower rose above the city like a mountain, or a gargantuan accusatory finger pointed at her innermost desires. She swooped down and landed on a sundial just on the outside of the structure.

She did not even have to enter the cathedral to spot the man she sought. She saw the unmistakable lion-headed walking stick before she even recognised Schindler, strolling the plaza outside the cathedral like a cat surveying its territory.

There were no hiding places in the massive plaza in which she could make her transformation. She had to wait until none looked her way before she flowed into her effortless metamorphosis. She made her way to Benedikt, who sat with ease on a bench. He tipped his hat in greeting as he stood. She did not understand why he felt the need to press her hand to his lips, but she committed the social custom to memory. "Have you waited for me every day?" she asked in wonder.

He offered her his elbow, and she took it. He guided her around the perimeter of the massive gothic structure, scarcely concealing his delight at the amazement on her face. There were birds aplenty in the city, but none that could appreciate the beauty of human ambition. "I estimated the amount of time to might take anyone to become aware of her own voyeuristic tendencies," he replied at long last. "But you are no ordinary woman. If your preferred form is that of a bird, the passage of human time might lose significance for you. If you wish to understand the world of human composition, it might serve you well to spend more time as your flightless counterpart."

She weighed his words.

"Where do you nest, songstress?"

For the first time, Ava felt self-conscious. She preferred to remain in nightingale form but had spent so much time in her human mind; she felt like a derelict for making her home in the wild and not having a proper address.

What was she to do to be a respectable lady in Vienna?

"I am inviting you to board in my home," continued Benedikt as if reading her thoughts. "It will not tarnish your reputation, should you wish to join the ranks of people. You can fly in through this small door and make your home in my study, either in a makeshift nest or on the pallet I have prepared for you. This is the

Age of Enlightenment, the Age of Reason! There is no better time for a lady to come into her own, or a composer like myself to draw inspiration from your songs."

Could she abandon her wild world and all of her innocence? She had already tasted the sweet music of the maestro and decided that she could never return to the primal woods.

Not wanting to draw the attention to the unfashionably odd clothing that always materialised around her curves, she transformed back to a nightingale when Benedikt alone was watching. She perched on his shoulder, Benedikt wound his way through the streets as if he owned them, the stars were beginning to appear, and oil lamps lit the cobblestone roads like tiny captive wishes.

His flat was far from opulent, but perfect in its symmetry and cleanliness, almost to the point of lifeless and mechanical. But the windows offered enough sunlight for her to pretend that she was free.

He beckoned her into the parlour. "Let me hear you sing, something of your creation that mortals can understand."

She closed her eyes, allowing her human larynx to

reimagine wild calls as human notes.

He was at once enthralled and thoughtful. "Your songs lack the structure that great composition requires. Try this…" He sat down at the pianoforte and played a simple melody. Her face flamed, but she knew that Schindler was right. She saw right away that it had symmetry and variations on small themes. It would never attract another bird with its predictability: it was blockish and lacking in spontaneity. But she was here to learn.

If he hadn't been correct in his assessment, then she wouldn't have been so drawn to Ludwig's genius, the sort of hubris that made the gods of Olympus jealous.

As the weeks went on, Ava became enmeshed in human experience. Benedikt not only taught her some compositions of his own on the piano, but also took her to see the city. He showed her works of art and pointed out the elaborate detail of the elaborate architecture. She delighted in gothic monstrosities, rococo splendour, and the new Empire style. There had been a time when she scarcely could have imagined putting forth that kind of effort just to build a nest, and yet now she could not bear to think of being deprived of such beauty all around her.

The nightingale woman was also exposed to less savoury aspects of humanity, with beggars and drunkards. Once she could have sworn she saw Herr Beethoven pelting from a tavern, and she trilled a cadence in a vain attempt to hail him. Benedikt drew an arm protectively around her shoulders.

She began to see her host, patron, and mentor in a different light. She started to notice the angle of Benedikt's jaw and the way that the harsh winter light played with the auburn curls of his hair. She wondered if her shape as a woman was as plain looking as her avian incarnation, and hoped that her voice pleased him, though she wasn't quite certain why.

This new concept of romantic tension—perhaps even the urge to mate—frightened her. One night after she retired to her room, she decided that she would retreat to her familiar bird's body, make herself as small as possible, and avoid the human dreams that now teased and whispered suggestions in the darkest corners of her mind.

She had done it all of her life. She would make herself feel very light, and half of her organs would vanish to make her body lighter. The world around her would seem to grow bigger as she shrank.

But the transformation was slow and painful this

time, and Ava was only able to sprout wings. So changed was she by these human experiences, she curled up in bed, tucked her head under her wing, and her only relief was that her avian voice box still worked the way a nightingale's should. She sang herself to sleep even as tears soaked her pillow.

🕊

...How is it that I burn for you, even as you continue to turn your sight skyward and never respond to my music? It is as if these notes have fallen upon deaf ears. Do you deliberately shun me when I sing your praises?

🕊

She was still trying to fathom human courtship in all of its public display when Benedikt presented her with two pieces of paper that read *Ludwig van Beethoven.*

"These are tickets to an *Akademie,* a benefit concert." Now that she had spent enough time with Benedikt, he was certain that her budding attraction for him would override her fascination with Beethoven, as she would see him through her human experience as slovenly and unattractive.

Benedikt presented her with a long, flowing blue gown fitted just beneath her bust, leather slippers, and a shawl made from the pelt of some animal. She shuddered and tried not to wonder what it had been; or worse, if it was any creature she had seen from her days in the woods. She straightened her neck and allowed the serving girl to help her into this strange, constrictive plumage of stockings and other under things, and finally let the girl pin her flowing hair into a fashionable coif.

Ava had never studied her reflection in a mirror before, but now she couldn't stop staring. Why, she looked like a lady in a painting! Perhaps she stood a chance of having a music career if she could learn to assimilate into society.

This time they took a carriage, and Ava did not find it strange. She was becoming accustomed to people who moved in every direction. The boxy carriage felt less like a cage than she had been anticipating, and the proximity of the animals ahead of her soothed her. Benedikt occasionally raised his cane at passers-by, and Ava imagined a miniature roar coming from the leonine handle.

The *Theater an der Wien* rose above Vienna like an ornate square mountain. And it was right along a river, which delighted her. She loved the juxtaposition of human opulence and nature. The façade was imposing: a gem of the Empire Style. She could not take her eyes off the statues of the four feathered people above the gate, especially of the boy holding a bird. Were they shapeshifters as well? Benedikt told her that it was a tribute to the opera of another composer named Mozart and ushered her through the entrance that would take them to an opera box.

She had never seen such an expansive space under a single roof. There were velvet seats everywhere, like a café or a parlour, but so many of them! The blue and white colours of the décor reminded her of a frozen winter landscape, not unlike the elements on the other side of the mighty walls. There was an inclined floor full of seated people, and at least four higher levels. Were all these people filling them really here to listen to music? Most exciting of all was the space in front that Benedikt had said was a stage, with assembling musicians tuning instruments she had never seen before. The entire spectacle was framed by an arch overhead like a gateway to some celestial world.

A familiar figure moved in an adjacent opera box. Ava was still new to human decorum, grabbing Benedikt by the elbow, pointing, and blurting out, "Who's that?" she asked. Several people turned their heads to sneer at her.

"That is Prince Lichnowsky," Benedikt whispered, hoping she would lower her voice. "He is one of Vienna's foremost patrons of the arts and is particularly fond of Beethoven." The noble was also a notorious serial philanderer, but Benedikt kept this to himself.

"I saw him outside the apartment," she announced. "Who would have thought that such a wretch of a man could be held in such high esteem?" This invited even more gasps and titters, but Ava was even more oblivious to this. Benedikt made a mental note to address her social graces next.

"Beethoven does not care for aristocracy," Benedikt murmured in her ear. "It is a trait that has not served him well. His third symphony was originally a tribute to Napoleon, but he has since repudiated his admiration after Napoleon occupied Vienna."

"Well, we have no king of birds, and we do just fine," Ava proclaimed with a natural lilt. Benedikt's eyes met hers, stern and icy, but they crinkled at the corners.

"You will see that in some ways men are just mortals. Some are born into nobility, some can create music fit for the gods. Even our Ludwig came into his genius through a tortured early life that none could say was a childhood. But a true magician cares only for the enchantments he can capture…"

His words trailed off as a single scowling figure with dishevelled hair lumbered to the podium. At the sight of the maestro in his own element, Ava completely forgot about the man sitting next to her who had slowly tried to woo her over the weeks.

Beethoven raised the baton like a magic wand. The music began, and she felt the shockwave of emotion hit her body. All of those instruments played together like one voice. The myriad frequencies were new and exotic to her ever-expanding mind.

The highlight was terrifying and awesome in one moment, as the violins led with a harsh major third. The structure, which she could now identify, was so primitive, and yet such genius. It built in ferocity like a gathering storm until the sound suddenly dropped to the cadenza of a single oboe. This she understood, and she committed it to memory.

In spite of the multitude of bodies within the auditorium, the harsh winter cold was stronger than the collective body heat. Within the relative privacy of the opera box, Ava was delighted to discover that she could turn her mammalian body hair into downy feathers to insulate her beneath her finery. Beautiful as it was, it was not designed to withstand the elements. This extra layer of comfort allowed her to further lose herself in the concert.

The *Akademie* lasted roughly four hours, but she did not mind, other than that her newly enlightened human mind was nearly overloaded from all this new auditory information. She had never heard applause before, raining from all around like a storm, and she instinctively wanted to take shelter.

It was far from a perfect performance. Benedikt gave her a furtive sneer when the maestro had to stop and restart some of the numbers that appeared to have never before been rehearsed. If this was intended for Ava to see Beethoven's many flaws, it was ineffective. She loved him all the more for his human imperfections.

As the concertgoers began to file out, she locked eyes with Prince Lichnowsky and some sort of recognition registered in his eyes. He tried to make his way towards her, but she gathered her skirts and swept out of the doorway on Benedikt's arm. The composer had no time for him, so neither would she.

All the way back to her quarters, her thoughts whirled like spiral arms around the bulge of a galaxy. *Beethoven…Ludwig van Beethoven…*

...And yet, you sneer at royalty. I delight in this animalistic nature of yours, so much like my own, I fancy. It is a bone of contention among your peers, but I revel in it. I do not care for orderly ways, of fripperies and powders. Give me earth and sky and music. Give me your undivided attention, even if we are not meant to be...

Ava could not hide her distraction from her music lessons over the next few weeks. Try as she might to cage her warring emotions of longing, frustration, and even a dark rage for the futile time she had poured into trying to reach Beethoven began to surface. Benedikt was too shrewd a man not to notice.

"Come, little songbird, I have a proposition for you." Ava felt exhilaration over her recent breakthroughs in understanding the piano. How quaint that humans could only interpret music through such a barbaric system as a chromatic scale, unable to process melismatic warbles. But she was ready to feel some fresh air and consented to join Benedikt on a stroll through the Viennese streets. Snowflakes fell, fat as daisy petals scattering in fruitless divination.

"I dearly wish to meet this Beethoven," crooned Schindler. "But he'll be more likely to accept you as a piano student, as he loves both nature and beautiful women. I have found a liaison in a mutual acquaintance. Perhaps if I were to set you up with proper piano lessons with him, you might return the favour by way of an introduction?"

Ava knew she was no Aphrodite, but Schindler's silken tones washed over her. Benedikt may have stirred new feelings in her loins, but he was going to arrange a meeting with the man with whom she was still secretly obsessed.

Ava's heart was pounding as the servant led her into Ludwig's study. At long last she was finally in his presence in a way that he would understand. He rose from the piano bench to greet her. She had spent so much time as a nightingale, and later imagined him so much larger than life, that she was shocked to find herself a great deal taller than he.

The study was a chaotic mess, but no worse than the construction of natural nests. Her newfound human sense of smell recoiled slightly at his poor hygiene, but her animal mind took in other information: the scents of sorrow.

She smiled winsomely from the piano bench.

He did not know that she was a magical creature

and had no way of comprehending that she was capable of producing music praised by bards that he would never hear.

Her body was an airtight assembly of letters and words that he would never read, unheard notes densely clenched into a fist of passion.

She tapped into both natures, knowing that he could not hear her. But perhaps if she leaned in to press her cheek to his, he might feel the vibrations.

She called down the powers of her dual nature. Her warble had the beginnings of a simple birdsong but developing and recapitulating into true sonata form. And then she sang the oboe cadenza.

She felt him sigh.

"I heard that you had no childhood," she whispered. "I too, had no childhood. Like Aphrodite or Athena, we could be one with the gods…"

A shout from the doorway made her jump. Though Ludwig could not hear it, he felt her body tense and saw her obvious distress. He was on his feet before the door to his study flew open. Some madman dressed in rags, his face smeared with soot, charged master and student, brandishing a cane.

Ludwig, angered at this new intruder, grabbed the first piece of furniture within reach with which to defend his uncanny pupil. The chair went flying in her direction, and Ava ducked.

Her world exploded into an unfamiliar chaos of grown men battling all around her, and she never knew what hit her. She could not know that the maestro tried to protect her or that the attacker was still too quick, smashing her skull with the silver lion-shaped handle of his walking stick before the furniture knocked him aside. Just as rapidly as he felled the young woman, the intruder turned on his heel and ran from the building before any of the servants could stop him.

Only Ludwig witnessed the horror of his unknown nemesis and his dying prodigy.

"Pity, pity, too late…" she chirped. "They shall be your last words."

She interpreted Beethoven's scowl as a murderous glare at her, and the tides of her blood turned from longing to her instinctual vengeance. As her heartbeat slowed, she was in between lady and bird forms, appearing as something between a dark angel and a harpy.

She died with a thousand symphonies mute on her tongue.

And then her body dissipated, leaving only a huge question mark in the maestro's mind. She could have been a spectre or a hallucination. Only some of her spilled blood remained behind. Each series of droplets on the floor formed a pattern that one might decipher into a series of notes on paper.

Someone eventually did find the crimson traces of her death and transcribe her murder. She hid herself in the silences between the notes, the mute rage of her predecessor Philomela. Waiting to be resurrected by a cue from a baton, or perhaps a necromancer's wand, into a bloody crescendo.

...There is no other way that I can rid myself of my rival without vilifying myself in the history books. He has revolutionised the progress of music, rendering my own offerings archaic and pedestrian. But since no one will believe the nature of your existence, it is up to me to cut Beethoven to size. You have given me the power to take away something precious to him, to hurt him in a way no other man can. Perhaps he will now perish from grief. I am sorry that I must dispatch you, my Immortal Despised, but you played the part in my design quite well.

Eternally yours,
Benedikt

Everything was a blur to Ava after that. She *was*, and yet she *was not*. She remained in the house, which was nothing more than a spectral formation to her solid self-perception. She could not return to her bird form or fly, yet she found that she could drift from room to room like a dead leaf on a current. Occasionally she caught sight of herself in a mirror, not dressed as a Viennese lady of the Empire era, but in her earliest human form as a young woman in a grey gown, unbound hair trailing behind her on a non-existent breeze.

It was the way she had looked before she had developed an ego. But unlike those halcyon days, she could not release the burdensome trophies of her hard-earned pride, love, longing, and hatred.

The concept of time dissolved like a sugarloaf in the river. Curious groups of people trickled in and out of the building, which was now a tourist attraction. She tried to call out to them, but she might as well have been as mute as her ancestor, or the visitors as deaf as Beethoven.

She could not tell if she had been drifting for minutes or centuries when something sundered her from the house like a blade. Time began to speed up, and Ava saw things as they were: that the building was solid and she herself had been a disembodied spirit. When longing is severed from remembering, the space between the two becomes an infinitesimal void, smaller than thought and vaster than a secret dimension. It was through this gap she flew, not as a bird, but like a nonphysical feather sucked along a current.

The iron in someone's blood rang as clearly as a church bell, calling her to gather with some unseen congregation, yanking her into a room she had never seen before.

In the middle of a floor lay a mirror facing upward like the calmest waters. It doubled the light of the surrounding taper candles like thirteen pairs of flickering eyes.

The guttering light held in stark relief a mortal woman crouching by the mirror, motionless and fair as a painting, save for her trembling, bloody hands. She seemed so innocuous with her sweat-dampened brown curls resembling a row of violin scrolls, but there was a darkness about her that resonated in the nightingale woman like a tuning fork. As Ava floated closer to investigate, she saw that a dozen other spectres had arrived, all of whom were murmuring words of sweet vengeance.

Was this the reason for such an abrupt passage?

Ava had never been able to get her revenge after all these years. But why?

She's the one that Beethoven tried to save at Pasqualati House, whispered a muscular-looking wraith with a lupine grimace.

The great composer loved nature. He loved beautiful women, said another, dancing her way around the edges of the circle. *There was no way he was a suspect. They say that the mysterious attacker got away.*

It suddenly made sense to Ava why Benedikt had been adamant about meeting the composer to whom he could never measure up. She recalled a flash of jewelled red eyes in the silver lion's head.

For over two hundred years, she had remained tied to a location, waiting to exact revenge on an innocent man whose only crime was his inability to fit into a society fraught with vanities, his erratic behaviour stemming from the love he was so often denied. She could have defamed a legacy that had brought countless musicians together and given millions of ears unsurpassed beauty. Meanwhile, Schindler's scions were doubtlessly on the prowl, trying to ruin their own rival musicians.

Benedikt Schindler. The name she had not thought

of for centuries began to form silently on her cold tongue. The grief of Ava's revelations stirred her blood. She met the terrified blue eyes of the mortal witch who had summoned her. They were the same stormy hue as Benedikt's. Could this woman carry multiple dark lineages within her?

Some ponder the silence of a cage and call it art. Some bang on the piano and call it creation. Ava joined her spectral coven and called it a holy communion. Like her ancient forebear, she craved the taste of human flesh to even the score.

Her throat unlocked, and with a rage that stirred her roots all the way back to Philomela, she screamed a vengeance that surpassed any contemporary dissonance. There would be no final cadence, just resolution.

MUSE

THE BINDING

by Jasmine Jarvis

The threads of the Morrigan are woven within the tapestry of time. The thin red threads, like blood coursing through veins. Binding those who knew her, and those daring enough to cross her, to her dark heart for all eternity.

The blood of the Morrigan is their blood now.

The blood of the Morrigan and that of her coven has been spilt…

January 1850

The horsehair paintbrush pulls at the dark crimson clot on the palette, dragging it over to a dab of white oil paint. Mixing the coagulated colours to make the soft rose blush of my Muse's lips. I watch the colours blend, making sure to smooth out the lumps in the paint. The smell of turpentine from the rag and the small glass jar that balances precariously on the small wooden stool next to the canvas, fills my space. Yet when I peer out from behind the canvas, she is unaffected by it. I shiver, my breath suspended on the cold air as I let myself linger there in that moment, taking in her serene beauty. My Fairy Queen. The room is freezing, but I dare not turn on the heat as I need to keep her as she is. My Muse, resting on the daybed, clothed in a sheer nightgown, her long auburn hair brushed smooth, the tresses tumble down over her bare, alabaster shoulders. Her eyes are closed, her arms rest gently on her stomach, her beautiful dainty feet are slightly pointed, as though she is on tiptoe. Through the sheer gown, you can make out the slender shape of her legs.

My darling Muse.

I return my attention now to the canvas and begin to paint her exquisite Cupid lips. In my painting, her shining emerald green eyes are open, her lips slightly curve in a smile as she looks back at me from the canvas: the same look she would give me as I painted her when she was alive.

October 1849

I was desperate. Moving quickly along the cobbled streets of London, the scrap of paper in my hands with the address scrawled across it, given to me by a fellow artist in our building. I was never one to give to superstition, but I was desperate. She was leaving me. My Muse was going to leave me to return home to Scotland, and nothing I could say or do would make her reconsider. If she were to leave me, the success I have gained through painting her will go with her. Before her, I struggled to get my art noticed. No matter what I did, I just could not get into the Pre-Raphaelite Brotherhood. But when I saw her in Hyde Park, I knew she was mine. There is something about her. A magic that flows from her to me and onto my canvases. The moment I started painting her, my life changed. Suddenly, I was welcomed into the art community. I attended exhibitions where my portraits of her took pride of place. Now I was on the verge of making it as a member of the Brotherhood, and she had decided now she was going to leave me.

I turned down a narrow street, picking up my pace. My Muse was going to be on the train back to Loch Lay, and I needed help. I needed guidance. I leapt over the sludge and grime that pooled on the street, keeping my wits about me as I made my way through the slums of London. I avoided eye contact with the locals, moving quickly to avoid the children who would try to "bump" into me in the hopes to fleece my pockets. I struggled to contain my revulsion of the stench that surrounded me as I desperately searched the doors until I found the one I was looking for. Quickly running up the steps, I smoothed out my vest and coat, straightened my hat, and knocked on the door in the pattern advised to me by the artist back in the share house.

Two knocks. Pause. Two knocks. Pause. Three knocks. Pause. One knock.

I step back and wait. Inside, I can hear the pathetic mewl of a cat and a woman's voice telling it to hush. A click and the handle turned, the door opening wide enough, and the face of a crone peered out to look at the desperate man standing before her there on her stoop. Keeping my voice as low as possible so as not to draw attention from the people walking on the street behind me, I spoke to her, "Madame Grace, I need your help. I was given your details by…" Before I could finish, the chain dropped from its latch and the door opened. Madame Grace now motioning for me to enter. I stepped over the threshold and Madame Grace quickly closed the door behind me. A three-legged black cat sat on the bottom step and watched on. There was an unusual aroma in her house, a sickly-sweet smell that I could not place. The shift from the odour outside to the pungent odour of the clairvoyant's home caused my stomach to clench. I grimace, and all the while the cat watched my every expression. For a fleeting moment, I could believe that the cat would later divulge my reactions to Madame Grace when I was no longer there.

"Come. Follow me, I have been expecting you, Mister Byron Hetherington." Madame Grace turned away from me then and headed down the narrow corridor, her black gown swished about her feet, stirring up the layer of dust resting on the wooden floor. I follow her down to the back and into the parlour room. Moving quickly, she snatched the curtains shut, blocking out the gloomy London light from outside. I watched Madame Grave move about the room, turning the flicker of flame in the kerosene lamps up just enough to give the room a soft, warm glow. In the centre of the room was a small round oak table. A black lace tablecloth was draped over the tabletop and sitting in its centre was a crystal ball and a deck of tarot cards. "Sit," Madame Grace commanded, and I moved quickly over to the seat closest to me. The ticking of the large Grandfather clock in the front entryway echoed throughout the house. Madame Grace was now by the table with her back to me. I could hear her mumbling to herself. The walls were adorned with mounted taxidermy animals. Shelves crowded with jars, strange objects floating in the amber liquids. As Madame Grace stood there muttering to herself, I continued to let my eyes wander over the décor, however I was only able to make out fragments of the dark curiosities as the shadows cast by the lamps danced and shifted along the walls making it difficult to truly ascertain Madame Grace's decorative range.

Madame Grace fell silent and walked over to a set of shelves where she then took up a small clay urn. Removing the cork stopper, I watched on as she sprinkled something into the teapot that was sitting there. The steam rose from the teapot, only to be extinguished when she placed the lid back on. Madame returned the clay urn to the shelf before returning to the table, placing the teapot down next to the tarot cards, taking her seat now opposite me. She looked at me for a moment, making me feel uncomfortable—I was convinced she was reading my thoughts. Her right eyebrow arched, and her lips curled up at the ends in a sly smile. She was reading my thoughts! What was I getting myself into? I was going to take my leave right there in that moment—it felt like the walls of the room were now closing in on me and something powerful was lurking on the other side, I am most sure of it.

Pouring the steaming grey-violet liquid into a chipped teacup, she spoke softly to me, "You must not keep what does not belong to you. Especially one that is not of this world."

"I'm sorry?" I tried not to let my nervous stammer creep in.

"The girl. You want her to stay, but you must let her return home. It is time she returns home; she has been wandering in the wrong form for too long now. It would be wise not to interfere with the bonds of a family of the likes she comes from." The walls were closing in and I swallowed hard, trying to clear my mind because Madame Grace was tearing through my thoughts now like a hungry beast. "Please, drink this. It is a tea that will help open the channels of communication with the spirits. Consider it a show of good faith to the spirits wanting to communicate with you. It won't harm you." I looked down at the steaming liquid in the teacup. I was trying to place the acrid aroma, but Madame again insisted I needed to drink it now. I help my nose to avoid the smell and took a sip. Despite the awful smell, it tasted sweet, and after the first sip the temperature of the liquid cooled down rapidly, and I finished the brew without hesitation.

Placing the empty teacup back down on its saucer, I began to tingle from head to toe.

The room grew dark and Madame reached out across the table. Taking my hands in hers, she began, "You crave success and a spot within the Brotherhood. I see exhibitions and travels abroad with your art."

"Yes, but do you see her with me? My Muse?" She squeezed my hands, and just beyond her, I saw mists swirling, moving closer to her.

"No, she is not with you." I tense up. Madame frowned. "The others are saying do not touch her. Do not bring harm to this young woman, for you know not from whom she is descended—a powerful woman, a vengeful woman has been seeking her. For your own safety, you must let this girl go."

I felt a rage well up in my belly. "If I let her go, I will never make it to Paris! Before her, no one would look at my art, but when I paint her, my work comes alive! I am on the verge of making it to Paris. Please, there must be something I can do to make her stay with me. What if I were to reach out to her family and explain the situation?" I was desperate.

"Her family are all here with us now. They are imploring you to let her go."

I look around the dark room. It was just Madame

and me.

Madame opened her eyes and released her hold on my hands. The room felt flat. "Let her go. Holding on to her will be your undoing."

Air caught in my lungs and I felt like I was choking. This was getting me nowhere. *An ancestor calling my Muse back to her native Scotland? What rubbish!* "Thank you for your time, Madame Grace, but I feel I have to do what I can to keep her." I put the money on the table and stood up. As I tried to move by her, her right hand shot out and grabbed at my left wrist.

"You touch that lass, and you will pay a most terrifying price. Are you willing to lose your career? Are you willing to lose your *life*?"

I did not reply, instead pulling my arm free of her grasp, I walked out of the room and down the corridor and to the front door. Madame Grace did not follow me.

Out on the street, the cold winter air filled my lungs and my mind; free of that cursed place, I regained my focus. I will keep my Muse.

I will make her stay.

🕊

I set out the canvas, cleaning rags, oil paints, and

my best brushes. I move over to where she will be sitting for me, slightly adjusting the potted plants to better catch the light. Today she will become my Fairy Queen, standing in the Garden of Eden. I had two more paintings to complete before my exhibition in six months' time—the exhibition that will be my debut as a member of the Pre-Raphaelite Brotherhood. I would be moving in the same circles as my idol, the founder of the Brotherhood—William Holman-Hunt. I agonise over every brushstroke, every little detail, and before I found my Muse, I really struggled. With her, it is like she has a magic about her because when I began to paint her, my work changed. Every painting, every sketch, it was like we were connected.

A thin red thread wrapped around my heart.

A sharp pain hit my stomach. She would be leaving me. She told me so. Back to Scotland. In my mind, I replayed that conversation.

"Why? Why now, when we are so close to achieving amazing things?" I asked her.

"I can't explain. I just have a feeling in my heart that I need to go home."

The door to my studio creaks open and I know she is standing there watching me prepare the set.

I do not speak. My throat clenches tight, forcing

the anger back into my belly. My Muse approaches, knowing what I need from her without saying anything. She disrobes and moves by me and when I look up, she stands before me naked. The emerald green leaves of the plants and her long auburn hair are all that covers her modesty. She is beautiful. There in that moment stands pure perfection. Clearing my throat and forcing a smile through the despair I had been drowning in, I greeted her.

"So glad you could make it. Today we will continue to work on the Fairy Queen. I will need to plan the schedule for the other two pieces left to finish so we get them down in time for the exhibition."

"But I told you I am lea—"

I hold my hand up to her. "Stop. You can still change your mind."

I move behind the canvas, select a brush, and swish the horsehair in the emerald green oil paint. I dab at the canvas, a bit too hard. I force myself to slow down. I refuse to make eye contact with her. For the rest of the day, we are silent. She poses without complaint while I paint my Fairy Queen wearing a crown of roses atop her auburn hair, her gossamer wings shimmer with every brush stroke.

By evening, the anger festered to where I was now

wound tight. She dressed while I cleaned the brushes. I watch her move, effortless, so much grace in the smallest movement of her form. I knew that I had to act now. I had no choice if I were to make it into the Brotherhood. She will see how great we are together. I place the brushes down onto the pile of cleaning rags, taking up a piece of cord I had used to tie back a curtain earlier, I quietly approach her from behind. Turning now to face me, her eyes flashed in fear.

"Please! No! Don't do this!"

I grab her as she turned to flee. Forcing her down, I wrap my hands around her slender throat and press down as hard as I can. I pressed against her airway and waited until she stopped moving. Pressed down and waited until the light left her green eyes and her breath left her lungs. I thought I had heard her utter a name:

"Isobel."

I held a small hand mirror in front of her slightly parted rosebud lips. There was no air. There was no life left. She was mine now for good. I gently touch her neck, tracing the flourish of the dark scarlet bruises with my fingertips. I can cover those up. I move now to complete my plan. I place a blanket from my bed onto the floor next to her. Lifting her tiny form, I lie her down on the blanket and wrap her up. It was a

Friday evening, and I knew that the other artists in the share house were all out at the taverns.

They were not as dedicated to art as I.

Down in the basement was the next step to my plan. I pick my Muse up, the ends of the blanket cover her auburn crown and dainty feet. We leave my studio and head down to the basement.

In the cold, dank basement, I lay her down on the bench before running back up the stairs to lock the door. I return now to my Muse, peeling the blanket away and then removing her clothes. I wash her clean, preparing her for eternal beauty. Forever my Fairy Queen. I force myself through the embalming process, draining her of her blood, cleaning out her torso, and packing it with rags and sawdust. In the corner of the basement, I had a vat of paraffin wax and other preserving fluids, melted down and ready to seal her in eternal beauty. I gently pull her hair up into a chignon before using a crudely made corpse stand to hold her upright. I make sure to take great care with the whole process. I slowly apply the wax so as not to have it run and pool in patches. Making sure to position her limbs just so for our future portraits.

Giving her a flawless finish.

In doing this, she will be with me forever. I will be

able to paint her forever. I will have my exhibition and my induction into the Brotherhood. Once completed, my Muse stood before me. Mine forever. I sat on the bottom step and waited for the wax to set. I waited there with her and justified my actions until the early hours of the morning.

Shrouded in the blanket, I carry her back up to my studio. I open the windows to allow the winter air in to keep the wax set. I return to the basement to finish cleaning up. Scrubbing any spots of blood. It took a few trips with the pail to empty the large vat I had used to collect the blood. Tipping the now coagulated blood and organs down the drain there in the back alley behind the share house. Making sure no one was passing by. The bloodied rags and equipment I bundled up in a canvas sack, and in the corner of the basement cut into the stone wall was a storage space, about six-foot high by three-foot wide and five-foot deep. Placing the sack inside the cavity, pushing it all the way to the back, I close the door, securing it with a padlock that I had bought earlier. No one would go looking. The vats of paraffin wax and embalming fluids, I managed to drag over to the far corner of the basement. I made sure the lids to the wax and embalming chemicals were secured tight before returning to my studio for another day of painting my Muse.

Unable to use the fireplace in my studio, I froze as I painted. But it was worth it to have her with me. Every day was a joy to wake up to see her standing there. Never to leave me. Pure perfection. My final pieces for the exhibition were now almost done. In my sleep I would dream of the moment I would accept my place in the Brotherhood, becoming a Pre-Raphaelite artist known the world over. As I would paint, I would talk to her. We would discuss our plans. Once I made enough money, I planned on us moving to a nice house just outside of London. I wanted a place where we could not be disturbed, and I told her so every day.

"Just you and me, my darling Muse."

Whenever I discovered cracks in the wax, I would run down to the basement where I would melt some of the stored wax and then carefully coat over the spots. All the while I would assure her, she was ever so perfect. When I finally finished the last piece for the exhibition, I celebrated by going out with the other artists for a night in London. I placed her in my wardrobe, shrouded under my coats and scarves. Shortly after I had embalmed her, I had changed the lock on my studio just in case the landlady was to go snooping—the other artists said that she would go in and take pieces of art as payment if tenants fell behind in their rent. While I was not behind in my rent, I did not want to take the chance that she would think to help herself to one of my paintings for the exhibition (and finding my Muse in the process).

The night was spent moving from one tavern to the next. The pressure was lifted, and I was giddy with the impending success that was coming my way. In the rising morning sun, bleary and ready for sleep, I unlocked the door to my studio and stumbled into my room, kicking the door closed behind me. Moving towards the bed, I realised the wardrobe was open and my clothes were thrown all over. I was most certain that I did not leave my studio earlier that evening in such a state, and the door was indeed locked when I returned moments earlier. The rest of my studio remained untouched. My heart quickened as I approached the open wardrobe. I peer inside to see her standing there as I had left her.

A cry escapes me and I fall backwards when looking at her face, I realise that *her eyes are now open.*

How can this be? Horrified, I stare at her, at her once green eyes that are now cloudy white in death.

She is staring right at me.

Maybe the wax had worn off, and I had not

noticed. Maybe it was the drink getting the best of me? Yes, that was it. I was sure it was the drink. A good sleep will set everything right again. I pick up the coats that lay about the floor and put them back in the wardrobe, closing the doors and turning the key.

I locked the wardrobe before I left —

A feeling of unease settled in my stomach. I tuck the key in my waistcoat pocket and then lay down in my bed; the alcohol pulling me into a deep sleep.

April 1850

I wish I could say that was the only strange thing that had happened, but the energy has shifted in my space and I find myself being tormented by my actions. Tormented by her. As my exhibition draws closer, no longer do I dream of that moment of acceptance into the society I so crave. Instead, I see her. My Muse. She is standing there in the gallery, the wax now melting and revealing her decaying flesh. She stands there in these dreams and she cries. Each sob is a knife plunging right into my chest. "You should have let me go. Now she is here." She would wail as everyone else in the gallery stared in horror. I would wake from these nightmares in a sweat and I would check the wardrobe. No matter how many times I apply the wax, her eyes are always open, and she stares at me.

I woke from the nightmare where she was strangling me there on the floor of the gallery while guests cheered her on, to find my studio in a complete mess. When I started having these nightmares, I had moved my art for the exhibition out and into the gallery for fear of them being destroyed. This course of action to protect my work seemed to anger the presence that had now taken hold. Paintbrushes would be snapped in half, new canvases cut to ribbons. My clothes were torn and covered with paints.

Every morning I would wake from these nightmares of my Muse to find the name *Isobel* repeatedly scrawled across the walls in red paint.

Every morning I would find a jackdaw perched on my windowsill—at its feet lay the bloodied and mangled body of a hatchling pigeon.

And then there are the thin red threads.

Thin red threads began to protrude from her. Through the stitches, the wax.

Then the thin red threads started to come out of me and pulling on them was unbearable. An itch in my left eye was from the tip of a thin red thread poking out from the tear duct. With my hands trembling, all I can do is snip the thread off as close as possible to my eye, but it still itched. I cannot take this anymore. I had stopped sleeping. I stopped eating. I was afraid to leave the studio for fear she would follow me. I had to stay in the studio with her. All my art supplies she has destroyed. My exhibition and debut as the newest member of the Brotherhood was now less than a week away. I sit here in my room with her, her white eyes bore into me, and I can hear her in my head in my waking hours now. In my nightmares she screams as she embalms me alive, right there on the gallery floor where I watch my blood spill out of me, in a tangle of red threads that run up and into her throat where my hands had once squeezed the life from her. Now there is no one watching. It is just us in the gallery, surrounded by paintings of her.

My Muse. My horror.

The morning of my exhibit, I sit on my bed and stare into the wardrobe at my Muse. Her white eyes watch my defeated form. I am hunched over. At the open window behind me I hear the jackdaw arrive, no doubt bringing with it another dead hatchling. Red threads are protruding from underneath my fingernails, pulling on them causes excruciating pain. I can hear her whispering rhymes—old Scottish rhymes—and chants. I hold my hands over my ears, but it is no use—she is in my head. I must stop this. My exhibition is in a couple of hours. I stand up and move to the wardrobe; slipping my arms around her waist, I lift her corpse out of the wardrobe, repulsed as my fingertips graze against ice-cold rotten flesh now exposed through the gaps of wax—I had stopped repairing the cracks a while ago now. I quickly wrap her in a blanket and check to see the landing is clear before taking her down to the basement. I planned to lock her in the space in the wall and leave her there for good. This way I would escape my Muse's torment. I would make the exhibition tonight and my career as an artist will take off. Hurrying now, I carry her down the staircase and down to the back of the house, to the basement. I move quietly so as not to wake others, closing and locking the door behind us, I run down the stairs, stopping once reaching the basement floor where I saw *her*.

My Muse.

My brain could not process what I was seeing. Before me she stood, alive and in the clothes she had been wearing the last night she drew breath. She was not smiling though, her face was dark, her mouth contorted in a sinister grimace. The body in my arms fell to the floor, the thud drawing my attention down to the floor. The blanket revealed a body that was not hers. I kneeled to take a closer look. It was covered in wax, but the cracks revealed a substance that appeared to be clay. And the face—the face was *mine*. I was looking at an effigy of *me*. When I looked up again, my Muse remained on the other side of the basement, still watching me. I realised then that the bench was set up with bloodied rags and tools that I had once used.

On her.

At the end of the bench was the vat that had once held her blood and organs, and at the other end, the vats of paraffin wax and embalming fluids—the chemical smell was overpowering and I felt dizzy. I stand up and slowly move back up the stairs. The red threads are now spreading across the floor towards me. My Muse is then joined by another woman. An older woman.

"Isobel Gowdie. The Witch of Auldearn."

I hear my Muse say.

"You should have let me go, foolish, foolish man!"

Present Day

Over time, the home had changed owners and purpose. The mystery of the missing artist and his Muse lingered in the background. The story went that the artist, so desperate to make it in the Pre-Raphaelite Brotherhood, was overcome with the pressure and he snapped—disappearing into obscurity. His beautiful Muse, the Fairy Queen in all his paintings, was believed to have returned to her home in Scotland. Although some (the other artists that lodged in the house at the same time as Mr Hetherington) believed she suffered a more sinister fate.

The reported sightings of a slight, beautiful auburn-haired lass who would appear and then disappear in the room that had once been the studio of the artist did not deter Izzy when she moved in. In fact, this house—she believed—with its paranormal stories, would be a good conduit for what she was hoping to achieve. Izzy moved in and began her preparations…

In the studio the Muse remained bound by Isobel Gowdie—her punishment for not returning to Scotland—a promise agreed to by the fae in return for Isobel lifting the veil, allowing her to venture out into the land of humans. Taking the form of beautiful women over time, each one would captivate men and serve her well. She found she loved humans; they were so…simple. The Muse would move from body to body, for Isobel had made it clear that in human form, the fae can die. She had to be careful. She also had to return to save Isobel from trial as she had agreed to, but at the time the affections of a young man were stronger and the fae had left Isobel to languish in prison, enduring unspeakable torment at the hands of the witch hunters. By the time the Muse met the artist, she knew he could see who she really was, but not understand it and this excited her. Thinking it was his artist "eye" he depicted her in his art as his Fairy Queen. She grew fond of him, and their bond flourished through his painting. Eventually though, his own dreams and desires were greater than her and she wanted to return to her kin.

The night she died was the night Isobel found her—through the pain of a human death. And Isobel was ready to seek revenge for the fae's betrayal. As punishment for abandoning her, Isobel bound the bodies of the Muse and her artist and entombed them within the walls of the basement. Entombing the Muse in her ghostly form in the house for all eternity.

Drops of blood and wax bring the family back together. Izzy was now staring at the ghost of her beloved Enzo, while upstairs in the studio the Muse was looking at the glowing ember eyes in the dark corner of the room—a face emerging, one she had not seen in such a long time. Isobel moved forward, a smile on her face.

"Do you want to go back home, my dear Queen?"

The Muse nodded.

"Then I need that girl and you are to help me. When I have her, I will make sure the Devil releases you from this place."

"You promise?"

The Witch of Auldearn smiled.

"I promise."

The door of the studio opened, and the Muse could hear the voices of Izzy and Enzo trail up the stairs. She followed Isobel Gowdie over the threshold.

ENZO

THE BROKEN AND
BLOODY CONSEQUENCE

by Jodi Jensen

"Enzo?" Izzy's breath caught in her throat as she stared at the ghost of her beloved. "Is it…" She reached her hand towards him. "It's you, it's really you."

His narrowed gaze locked on hers, and his lips stretched in a grim line.

The hairs on her arms rose, and she shuddered at the sudden chill emanating from him. "I did it. We…we did it." She took a step back, grimacing at the visible cuts on his neck, bare chest, and arms. Cuts she'd made. "Say something, baby."

Floating closer, he scowled at the blood and wax-covered mirror on the floor while behind him, the other orbs drifted away, all but one.

A woman, hair loose around her shoulders, wearing a gauzy gown of grey silk, unhinged her jaw and let loose a scream of unearthly rage before darting away after the others.

Shuddering, Izzy knew she should be worried about those other orbs, but all her focus was on Enzo. It'd been two weeks since the funeral, two long, heartbreaking weeks since she'd seen his body laid out at the wake.

Seeing him now, she longed to embrace him, but in his current form, that wasn't an option.

Her gaze broke from him long enough to flicker to Isobel's grimoire. Maybe there was something in there she'd missed, something to bring his spirit back to his body.

In the blink of an eye, Enzo stood between her and the book, shaking his head.

"But—we need to try," she pleaded. "I need to hold you again." She took a step towards the grimoire.

A blast of frigid air hit her smack in the face, stealing her breath and forcing her back.

"What the—" She tried again, but this time was tossed across the room, bouncing off the wall like a rag doll.

Enzo hovered over her, his eyes filled with

sadness, his face stern and unyielding.

She tried to get up, but a sharp pain in the back of her head stopped her cold. Lifting a hand, she touched the sore spot, her fingers encountering a sticky wetness. As she brought her hand away, she gasped at the sight of her own deep red blood coating her fingertips.

"Why," she choked, blinking up at Enzo. "Why'd you…"

Her head swam and her stomach twisted as bile rose in her throat and warm fuzzy darkness enveloped her.

❧

"Oh my God…" Izzy pulled on the loose end of twine and unwrapped the burlap to reveal the grimoire. The small, brown, leather-bound book was ragged around the edges, the pages yellowed with age.

With all the reverence of an awestruck nun, she opened the book.

"Enzo, look."

Sitting beside her, he leaned in close, his own voice hushed. "Is that Gaelic?"

"Aye," she said, smiling as she carefully turned a few pages.

"And you're sure it's Isobel's?"

Her smile grew as she pointed out her ancestor's

name, Isobel Gowdie, signed with a flourish at the bottom of a page near the front. "Aye," she said again, running her fingers over the centuries old ink. She turned the pages, one after another, scanning each one. "It's an account of dreams, visions, and encounters she had with the 'old folk'. Right here," she stopped at a passage midway through the book, "she's telling about feasting under the local faerie hill with the king and queen of faeries."

Enzo rested his chin on her shoulder, listening with rapt attention as she recounted the story Isobel had written.

"And here, she's talking about a water bull and being afraid of it."

"What's a water bull?"

"I'm not sure," Izzy admitted. She turned a few more pages until she came to a section with the heading Beneficial Magic. "Ah, here we are." Holding her place with her finger, she turned the pages, counting under her breath. "...Twenty-six, twenty-seven. Holy shit, twenty-seven charms and spells, direct from Isobel!"

"Brilliant!"

The excitement in his voice made her turn in time for his lips to meet hers in a celebratory kiss.

"Mmm..." She pulled away and grinned. "Let's see what else is in here."

"As you wish, love, but we're going to celebrate properly later." His eyes sparkled with promise, warming her heart, and lighting a flutter of awareness between her legs.

But even thoughts of his skilled lovemaking couldn't detract her from the discovery of the grimoire, and she turned back to the open book.

Her gaze landed on the first of the charms. "Look, a ritual to divert sickness from a child." She stumbled over some of the ancient Gaelic but managed to get the gist of it. "Oh wow, so, the illness is cast from the child, onto its cradle belt, then transferred to a cat or dog. Amazing!"

"Do you think it really worked?" Enzo padded to the fridge, then returned with a can of pop. "Does it say how, exactly?"

"I'm sure it does, but it's not the spell we're looking for." She flipped to another page, then another, scanning the words until she came to a series of thirteen pages titled Summonings. "This is it, it's got to be!"

🦋

The air around Izzy swirled with a hazy mist,

Gaelic mixed with English, and a cloaked figure drifted within the shadows. When she tried to move, something pressed down on her chest.

"Stay put," an unfamiliar female voice demanded.

Squinting into the blurred figure's face, a needle-sharp pain seared Izzy's eyes, and she let out a tortured scream. Her body jolted, and she fought against an unnatural darkness seeping into her skin.

"No!"

Enzo's rage-filled declaration penetrated the foggy miasma surrounding her, and she blanched as his translucent spirit collided with the dark orb, ripping the force away from her.

Her head lolled to the side, and the room faded to black.

After days of poring over the summoning rituals, and painstakingly translating the old Gaelic, Izzy gathered the needed items for the ceremony.

The first, and most important, was the athame. Made of pure silver and measuring nine inches, the etching of the phoenix at the top of the hilt symbolised rebirth, regeneration, and a new life. Black beeswax candles, unburnt, virgin olive oil, a length of braided hemp, and six silver bowls were easy enough to find. It was the herbs that required some looking. Agrimony, rue, and valerian were all essential to the ritual.

A local occult shop, Earthly Awakenings, ordered the custom athame, rue, and agrimony for her, while supplying the rest of the items from its in-store stock.

Finally, nearly a month after finding the grimoire, Izzy was ready to perform the ritual that would bind Isobel's soul to her own, allowing her to harness the powers of the long-dead witch.

They waited for the next full moon, then set everything in place. Izzy carefully measured and drew her pentagram, nine feet across, on the floor, then set a tall black taper in a silver holder on each point. She set the rue and valerian to steep in one cup, and the agrimony in another, then prepared the summoning candle by warming the tip of her athame and carving her name around the top half, Isobel's around the bottom half, and marking a broken line in the middle. When she finished, she tied a piece of the braided hemp around the candle and set it on a silver platter in the centre of the pentagram. Her stack of six silver bowls sat waiting next to the candle.

As the clock approached midnight, Izzy opened the curtains and windows, letting the unfiltered moonlight spill into the room.

"Are you ready?" she asked, holding a hand out to Enzo.

"I-zzzzzy…"

The sound of her name being called penetrated the fog in her mind. Izzy stirred and tried to sit up, only to find herself pinned to the floor by the ankles and wrists. She fought against restraints she couldn't see, her heart thrumming heavily.

"I-zzzzzy…"

She stilled at the long, drawn out taunt. The voice, little more than a whisper, came from directly above her. Closing her eyes, she centred herself, focusing her energy on her sight, willing herself to see the unseen. When she opened her eyes, a figure hovered above her.

A woman, brown hair tied up atop her head, sharp blue eyes in an otherwise plain face. She wore a traditional full length *léine* with an overskirt and long brown woollen cloak.

"Isobel?" The word tore from Izzy's throat, her disbelief evident, even to her own ears.

The woman tilted her head, eyeing Izzy with a mixture of menace and pity.

An unnatural stillness filled the air, as if the world around her was collectively holding its breath—

Isobel smiled.

A jolt zinged through Izzy, and her body seized. She couldn't move, but her mind was fully aware as the spirit of her ancestor infiltrated. She saw her own light leaving, beginning with her hands, travelling up her arms, and floating away, chased by darkness.

Memories filtered into Izzy's mind: images of taking a child's corpse from the ground and using it for a spell, creating effigies of the male offspring of her enemies and manipulating them to cause pain, suffering, even death, and finally, having carnal relations with the devil himself while letting him put his mark upon her shoulder and suck her blood.

Izzy screamed, fighting to block the memories gifted to her by the darkest of dark magic. Her body seized again—then once more, the accompanying pain piercing her nerves and making her body feel like it was on fire.

A single tendril of light snaked its way into her mind, wrapping around her and pushing the darkness from the core of her being.

Enzo—it had to be.

The wisp of light grew, driving the dark spirit further away as it moved through her.

Isobel gave a guttural roar, a string of Gaelic

curses spewing from her as she was, once again, denied her possession.

Izzy's body heaved in relief, and this time the darkness that engulfed her was peaceful.

"Promise me one thing."

Izzy looked up from the grimoire and smiled at Enzo. "Anything."

"If this goes bad, if something goes wrong, tell them it was suicide."

She recoiled from his words, her lips tightening into a frown. "What do you mean—if it goes bad? It won't—"

"It might—"

"It won't!" Leaning over, she planted a gentle kiss at the corner of his mouth. "I won't let anything go wrong."

He cupped her cheek, his forehead resting against hers. "I know you won't, but if it does—" He kissed her quick, forestalling her protest. "If it does, promise me, you'll say it was a suicide."

"Enzo—"

"I mean it, Izzy. Promise me, or I won't let you use my blood."

A flash of anger welled in her chest but was

squashed by her love for the man in front of her, earnestly pleading with her to cover her own ass. "Okay," she finally relented. "IF anything goes wrong, I promise to say it was a suicide."

He yanked her against him, wrapping her in a warm bear hug and whispered into her hair, "Thank you, my love."

Pulling away, her smile returned. "Can we get started now?"

Izzy opened her eyes in time to see a chair come flying at her, only to be diverted at the last second and smash into the wall beside her.

"Ye're strong, I'll grant ye that." Isobel's spirit was as clear as Enzo's now, and Izzy caught the malicious humour in the quirk of the witch's lips. Her gaze went to the mirror on the floor, and with nothing more than a slight nod of her head, it rose and hovered in the air. "But nay as strong as me."

Enzo's ghost floated in front of Izzy, his back to her as he faced off with Isobel. "I'm strong enough."

His voice held no trace of doubt, and if Izzy could've moved, she'd have rejoiced at his declaration.

"We shall see." Isobel twirled her finger, and the mirror followed suit, spinning faster and faster until the candle flung across the room, hitting the herbal storage case with a smash. The mixed scents of dried herbs filled the air, along with the witch's laugh.

Izzy didn't dare take her eyes off the mirror though as it continued to spin in the middle of the room. Enzo didn't have the magic, she did, and she was helpless to use hers. Mesmerising patterns of refracted light moved in circles on the ceiling, drawing her attention to the juxtaposition of beauty in the horror of the moment.

Enzo's energy vibrated around her, tense, protective, and aggressive as he stared her ancestor down. "I won't let you have her."

"Ye can't stop me," Isobel was swift to reply. She flicked her fingers, and the mirror exploded, raining shards of glass throughout the room.

Izzy screamed.

Izzy gave Enzo the valerian and rue tea to drink while she lit all the tapers.

"You could've at least sweetened it." He grimaced after a tentative taste. "This shit is nasty."

"I prepared it according to the requirements in the ritual." She rolled her eyes as he frowned at the cup. "Bottoms up, baby."

Downing the drink in a few huge gulps, Enzo wiped the back of his hand across his mouth. "Now what?"

"Take off your shirt and sit here on the floor"—she indicated the centre of the pentagram—"cross-legged, palms facing up on your knees. Close your eyes and clear your mind. And let me know when you feel relaxed."

"How about when I feel silly?" He grinned and yanked the shirt over his head, then wadded it into a ball, and tossed it across the room. "Shall I let you know that, too?"

"Clown," she muttered, stifling a giggle. Picking up her athame, she walked around the outside of the pentagram, passing the blade over the top of each flickering candle. Next, she stepped inside, and this time, held the tip of the knife in each flame, chanting a single Gaelic word three times at each stop. "Gairm, gairm, gairm."

When she finished, she sat across from Enzo, knife in her lap, and waited. Her excitement built as she watched his body relax. His shoulders drooped slightly, his wrists lay limp on his knees, and utter peacefulness blanketed his aura.

He opened his eyes and gave her a slight nod.

Izzy passed the second drink to him, the agrimony. "Drink it quickly," she said softly, not wanting to disrupt the mood.

Enzo swallowed the contents of the cup in three large gulps.

"Now, lie down next to the candle, feet facing west." She waited until he was settled. "Are you ready?"

"Ready." He closed his eyes as she approached, athame in hand. "And don't stop if I flinch, just do what you need to do."

With a final glance at the grimoire, she began.

Izzy's body was on fire. Still unable to move, she could only lay helpless, sliced to ribbons with pieces of the shattered mirror embedded in her flesh.

She frantically searched her mind for a counter-spell that would free her from her bonds, and the Gaelic word for "release" popped into her head. "*Schoileadh.*" The first time it came out little more than a whisper, the second time, a bit stronger. "*Schoileadh!*" She heaved a deep breath, preparing to shout, when a vice-like grip clamped down on her throat.

"*Bi sàmhach!* Ye will speak nay more." Isobel's voice held a note of grudging admiration as she hovered above Izzy.

"Enough!" Enzo roared, his spirit darting towards Isobel.

With an annoyed glance, the witch uttered a hurried phrase in Gaelic. *"Bi air falbh leat!"*

Though the words halted Enzo's progress, he fought against an unseen force holding him back. "I will not go away!" he declared, features tight with fury.

Isobel's dark gaze flickered to the far corner of the room. *"Thoir air falbh e."*

The ghost of a young woman with long auburn hair and alabaster skin sprang into view, blocking Enzo. Her lips moved as she chanted softly, her voice so low, Izzy couldn't make out a single word.

With Enzo out of her way, Isobel turned back to Izzy. "Ye summoned me, and I came, but ye dinna command me. 'Tis *I* who commands *ye*."

Izzy shuddered as the witch reached out to touch her, recoiling in shock when she felt Isobel's hands on her flesh. *Am I dead?*

"Ye ar'na dead yet, but ye will be." Isobel's lips curved into a wicked grin. "Dead in the way that matters, as I will possess ye."

Helpless to do anything but endure, Izzy watched as Isobel dipped her hands into the blood pooling around her, smearing the crimson liquid over her face, neck, and arms.

The witch chanted in a strange language; the words, low and guttural, sounded as if they were being ripped from her body. Her eyes rolled back in her head as she pressed her hands against Izzy's chest.

From the other side of the room, the young woman joined in the witch's lament.

Suddenly, Enzo's face appeared above Izzy, and three words whispered in her ear.

"Let me in."

Gaze locking with his, she uttered the Gaelic word for enter. "*Cuir a-steach*."

Izzy gasped as hands squeezed her heart, cutting off her breath in the space of a second.

"I'm sorry, my love."

Isobel's eyes flew open, her gaze pitch black in her blood-covered face. "Ye canna have her!"

The young woman appeared next to Enzo, her hands pulling on his, even as his squeezed tighter around Izzy's heart.

Her body seized. She struggled for a breath she couldn't find. Her final gaze locked on Enzo, his face tight with rage, his eyes filled with love.

Izzy placed her silver bowls at the collection sites, then lit the summoning candle, focused on Isobel, and held the knife in the flame as she chanted, "Gairm, gairm, gairm." With a quick flick of her hand, she sliced from the inside of Enzo's elbow to his wrist, letting the blood flow freely into the bowl. She repeated the process on the other arm, then moved on to his neck.

She frowned at the drawing in the grimoire, showing the sacrificial cut to begin just below the earlobe, slant across the neck, and stop at the inner end of the clavicle bone. Working fast, she made both slashes. She cringed at the volume of crimson that flowed from the wounds while marvelling as the blood followed the pre-ordained path and streamed directly into the bowls.

Other than a small gasp at the first slice across his neck, Enzo lay still, eyes closed, and sucking in deep breaths.

The last of the outlined cuts went from the bottom of the sternum, up and across the ribcage to the outer edge of the clavicle. And once again, the blood ran in smooth rivulets, collecting in the silver bowl.

Shutting her own eyes, Izzy recited the summoning chant.

Witch Isobel
Course through time
Oh, spirit come
I beckon thee
Come to me
Bind to me
Share thy power
Thy knowledge
Allow me
To do thy bidding

She opened her eyes and her gaze darted to each of the bowls, horrified to find them overflowing.

In the flickering candlelight, Enzo's skin had gone deathly pale. His chest rose and fell in rapid, shallow gasps, and when she reached out to touch him, his flesh was ice cold.

Her heartbeat thrashed in her ears as she tore her shirt off and clamped it over his neck, where the worst of the bleeding seemed to be.

"No—no, no, no," she screamed, as the blood soaked through the material. Her stomach lurched at the sight of dark crimson still running from his arms, but she didn't dare loosen her hold on his neck.

"Help! Someone help me!" She glanced around, her frantic gaze landing on the grimoire. She quickly scanned over the ritual, stopping cold when she saw part of a word that hadn't been there before. "Blood of a warlock" now read "Lifeblood of a warlock."

Wicked laughter filled her ears. "Enzo!" she screamed. "Wake up!"

A shadow appeared outside of the pentagram.

Izzy did the only thing she could think of and extinguished the summoning candle. The shadow, and the laughter, disappeared at once, leaving her alone with Enzo's body.

She stared at her blood-covered hands, still holding the soaked shirt tight around his neck.

"What have I done?" she whispered as tears slid down her face.

⸙

Locked in a vicious embrace with the ghostly young woman, Enzo was helpless to do anything but watch as Izzy's body lay motionless on the floor with Isobel hovering above her.

Suddenly, every candle blew out and an unnatural stillness once again blanketed the room.

Isobel's spirit slid into Izzy, unopposed.

He screamed, struggling to reach out to his

beloved.

Izzy's eyes opened, and she laughed—a throaty, evil sound. With a flick of her finger, he was ripped away and tossed into a deep, dark pit.

He'd failed.

Izzy was alive and possessed by the witch Isobel.

BIOGRAPHIES

1̃₃ DROPS OF BLOOD
IN ORDER OF APPEARANCE

JODI JENSEN, author of time travel romances and speculative fiction short stories, grew up moving from California, to Massachusetts, and a few other places in between, before finally settling in Utah at the ripe old age of nine. The nomadic life fed her sense of adventure as a child, and the wanderlust continues to this day. With a passion for old cemeteries, historical buildings and sweeping sagas of days gone by, it was only natural she'd dream of time travelling to all the places sparked by her imagination.

Twitter : @WritesJodi
Facebook : @jodijensenwrites

S.N. GRAVES earned her MFA in Popular Fiction from Seton Hill University and works as an editor and professor of genre fiction with a concentration in horror. Graves also writes under several pen names and creates art, including book covers.

Website : www.sngraves.com
Facebook : @Shannon.N.Graves

J.W. GARRETT is a multi-award-winning author. Initiated into fantasy after reading The Hobbit in elementary school, she has been hooked ever since. She writes speculative fiction from the sunny beaches of Jacksonville, Florida, but loves the mountains of Virginia where she was born. Her writings include novels, short stories, and poetry. Since completing Remeon's Crusade, the third book in her sci-fi fantasy series, Realms of Chaos, she has been hard at work on the next instalment. When she's not hanging out with her characters, her favourite activities are reading, running and spending time with family.

Website : www.jwgarrett.com
BHC Press : www.bhcpress.com/Author_JW_Garrett.html

BLACK HARE PRESS

KIMBERLY REI does her best work in the places that can't exist... the in-between places where imagination defies reality.

With a penchant for creepy shadows and hooks that leave you guessing, she can be found in anthologies from Black Hare Press, Eerie River Publishing, and Iron Faerie Publishing. She has taught writing workshops and edited novels for Authors You May Recognize.

Always on the lookout for new ideas, new projects, and new ways to make words dance, Kim is happiest behind a keyboard or doing anything at all with her beautiful wife.

Website : tales.studiorei.org/

M. SYDNOR JR. is an author of novels and short stories. He began his career in writing in 2005 after trading in his basketball sneakers for a pen and pad, and the desire to create worlds took off. Early in his writing journey, he learned there was more than just putting an idea to paper—you had to read. He lives in Northern California collecting an unhealthy number of movies, books and graphic novels. The characters of his fantasy series, The Legends of the World, take most of his time when he's not coaching high school basketball.

Website : msydnorjr.com

Twitter : @MSydnorJr

CHRIS BANNOR is a speculative fiction writer who lives in Southern California. Chris learned her love of genre stories from her mother at an early age and has never veered far from that path. Her stories have been published in over two dozen anthologies and range from horror and science fiction, to romance, fantasy, and steampunk.

When not writing, Chris enjoys musical theatre and road trips with her family.

Facebook : @chrisbannorauthor

Website : www.ChrisBannor.com

CRYSTAL L. KIRKHAM is a multi-genre speculative fiction author and podcaster. She has published several full-length novels and has been a part of multiple best-selling anthologies.
Originally from the west coast of British Columbia, she now chooses to call a tiny hamlet in central Alberta her home. She is an avid outdoors person, unrepentant coffee addict, part-time foodie, and companion to several delightfully hilarious canines.
Website : www.crystallkirkham.com
Twitter : @canuckclick

K.T. TATE is an English author inspired to write speculative fiction. She draws on her love of horror to explore the themes of cosmic and occult horror, the supernatural, folktales and witchcraft. Writing mainly drabbles and short stories, her works have been featured in a plethora of anthologies. All of which can be found on her website below.
Website : www.eldritch-hollow.com

DJ ELTON is a speculative author from Melbourne's west side who writes short stories, poetry and micro-fiction. She's had work published in anthologies and online literary sites with Black Hare Press, Paper Djinn Press, Aussie Speculative Fiction, Eleanor Merry Publishing, Barrio Blues Press, Iron Faerie Publishing and Little Quail Press. She also wrote a novella called The Merlin Girl. She likes writing medieval fantasy, dark fantasy and paranormal romance, as well as sci-fi robot stories. When not pushing a pen, she gets social, stays active, reads crime novels, collects paper and is involved in a few meditation-related non-writing projects.
Facebook : @djeltonwrites
Twitter : @djeltonwrites

BLACK HARE PRESS

NICOLE LITTLE lives in St. John's, Newfoundland, Canada. Her short stories have appeared in thirteen anthologies and her first novella, *The Lotus Fountain: A Slipstreamers Adventure,* launched in November 2020. In her spare time, Nicole has either a pen in her hand or her nose in a book. She is married with two daughters.

MAXINE CHURCHMAN is a grandmother from Essex, UK. Having always loved reading, she has recently discovered writing is fun too.

To pay the bills, she runs her own business selling promotional items and embroidered clothing to local companies.

She also enjoys hiking, caravanning, knitting and yoga.

Website : cccmaxine.blogspot.com

BETH W. PATTERSON was a full-time musician for over two decades before diving into the world of writing, a process she describes as "fleeing the circus to join the zoo." She is the author of the books *Mongrels and Misfits* and *The Wild Harmonic*, and a contributing writer to over fifty anthologies.

Patterson has performed in nineteen countries, expanding her perspective as she goes. Her playing appears on over two hundred albums, soundtracks, videos, commercials, and voice-overs (including seven solo albums of her own).

She lives in New Orleans, Louisiana with her husband Josh Paxton, jazz pianist extraordinaire.

Website : www.bethpattersonmusic.com

Facebook : @bethodist

JASMINE JARVIS is a teller of tales and a scribbler of scribbles. She lives in Brisbane, Australia, with her husband, Michael; their two children, Tilly and Mish; their German Shepherd, Ripley; and indoor fat cat, Dwight K. Shrute.

Twitter : @jjarvisauthor

Instgram : jasmine_jarvis_author

ABOUT THE PUBLISHER

BLACK HARE PRESS is a small, independent publisher based in Melbourne, Australia.

Founded in 2018, our aim has always been to champion emerging authors from all around the globe and offer opportunities for them to participate in speculative fiction and horror short story anthologies.

Connect
Website: *https://www.blackharepress.com/*
Twitter: *@BlackHarePress*

BLACK HARE PRESS

ACKNOWLEDGEMENTS

When we embarked on our Black Hare Press journey back in late 2018, we never envisioned the huge support we'd get from the writing community. We have been truly humbled by the number of submissions we've received.

So, thank you to everyone who crafted tales just for us—from the tiny tales in our Dark Drabbles series to these speculative stories in this 500 Fiction series—we thank you from the bottom of our hearts.

To our families and friends, collaborators, random strangers who took pity on us, and everyone who has helped us on the way: we couldn't have done it without you.

Special thanks to our Patreon supporters, especially James Aitchison, Jonathan Stiffy, and S. Jade Path. Take a look at the Patreon-only content and merch here—patreon.com/blackharepress—and consider helping us get to the next stage.

And to you, our discerning reader, we and these talented writers did it all for you. We hope you enjoyed these tales, and if you did, don't forget to leave a review.

Love & kisses

Ben & Dean

www.blackharepress.com

www.ingramcontent.com/pod-product-compliance
Lightning Source LLC
Chambersburg PA
CBHW050135120726
47903CB00002B/371